ABOUT THE AUTHOR

Jamie Rix is a television producer and director of comedy, and a comedy writer for programmes such as *Smith and Jones*, *Spitting Image* and *Comic Relief*. His first book, *Grizzly Tales for Gruesome Kids*, was shortlisted in the 9–11 category of the 1990 Smarties prize, and judged overall winner by the children's panel. *Fearsome Tales for Fiendish Kids* is his fifth book. Jamie lives in South London with his wife and two sons.

Fearsome Tales for Fiendish Kids

Jamie Rix

Illustrated by Ross Collins

*Hodder
Children's
Books*

a division of Hodder Headline plc

First published in Great Britain in 1996
by Hodder Children's Books

10 9 8 7 6 5 4 3 2 1

A Catalogue record for this book is available
from the British Library

ISBN 0-340-64095 2

Typeset by Avon Dataset Ltd, Bidford-on-Avon

Printed and bound in Great Britain by
Cox & Wyman Ltd, Reading, Berks.

Hodder Children's Books
a division of Hodder Headline plc
338 Euston Road
London NW1 3BH

Contents

For Charlotte, Jolyon, Sophie and Lisa
who are not all horrible

The Cat Burglar

Fedora Funklefink was a girl of exceptional talents, and all of them crooked. She was a first class forger who could imitate her mother's signature so precisely that even her mother couldn't tell the difference. She got off more games periods than any other person in the history of her school.

In one term, Fedora wrote notes from her mum saying she couldn't play netball because she had mumps, lumps, tummy bubbles, flat feet, sticky out ears, cartridge problems in her knees (*sic*), an excess of freckles, rotten teeth, Chinese flu and a tickly armpit. Woosh! Straight to matron – no sweat (and no freezing purple thighs either). In exams, she always came top by cheating. Not tiny cheats, like furtive

1

glances at her neighbour's answer, but huge, whopping cheats with mirrors, that had the whole school admiring her behind her back and started some of the smaller girls off on hopeless crushes.

But Fedora Funklefink was perhaps most famous for her money-making scams. At the tender age of four she had turned up at school with a packet of Polo mints in her pocket that her grandmother had given her in church the day before. She sold the mints per suck, charging four pence for a ten second licking and one pound fifty for a whole holey sweet. She had made seven pounds by the end of first break; twenty-one pounds fifty by the end of the day. The next day she bought seventy packets of Polos into school and made one pound thirty, which taught Fedora the lesson that often a good idea will only work once.

Her most enduring scheme was the charging of girls for the use of the toilets, insisting that they pay her one pound for de-spidering them. When girls complained that there weren't any spiders in the toilets, Fedora would exclaim, 'I know. That's because I do such a good job!' And if a girl still refused to pay, she would grab her collar and drop a spider down her neck until she did. Actually, they weren't real spiders. They were those spikey green stalks off the top of tomatoes, but if Fedora whipped them out of her pockets fast enough, the screaming girls couldn't tell the difference.

One summer holiday, Fedora was bored. At school there

were always a hundred girls she could hoodwink, but during the long summer break there was just her mum and her little brother, and her mum was far too canny to be rolled over and her little brother never carried cash, because he was only eighteen months old. So the opportunities for raking in the readies were scarce.

She tried washing the windscreen of her dad's car when he went to work in the morning and then not letting him out of the drive until he'd paid her two pounds, but he just laughed and drove over her foot. She tried knocking on old ladies' front doors and asking for donations to Help the Aged, but when they pointed out that they were aged and needed her help (so did she have any money that she could give to them?) Fedora ran away and hid in the park in case they gave her description to the police. She even tried setting herself up in the bicycle repair business, with a pot of glue, a box of plasters and a tin of tacks, which she scattered over the road to puncture the wheels of unsuspecting passing cyclists. Unfortunately, she had not read her newspaper, because on the very first day that she laid her tin tack trap, the Tour de France streamed through her village and three hundred bicycles slewed across the road in front of her house and squashed her mother's prize courgettes. Popular, she was not. Confined to her bedroom, she most certainly was.

One day, bored out of her tiny, scheming skull and kicking an empty crisp packet up and down the street,

Fedora Funklefink saw a handwritten notice pinned to a tree.

LOST CAT

Tiddles is a luvly cat who likes sleeping in the sun and chasing those fluffy white bits that you can blow off dandylions. She is my cat and I am very sad. becoz she has run away.

PLEESE HELP ME TO FIND HER

She is a mixed up sort of culler. Her paws are white and her tail is black and she's got a dyemond patch right in the middle of her fourhead. The rest of her is marmalayed (without the bits obviously).

THERE IS A REWARD OF £10 FOR ANYONE WHO BRINGS HER HOME!

Angela Tearful (9½)

At the bottom of the notice was a blurred photograph of something that looked like a cat, but could equally have been a dog or a jug of wine or a sphinx in the Egyptian desert. It was hard to tell really, but Fedora could smell a money-making scheme a mile off, and she tore the notice off the tree before anyone else could read it. Then she rushed home and dived into her wardrobe.

Several minutes later, Fedora was standing in front of her mum's mirror, admiring her hunting get up. Black leggings, black polo shirt and a black bobble hat that she pulled down over her face so that people wouldn't recognise her. Peering out through the fuzzy gaps between the stitching, she rummaged through her toy cupboard and found an old shrimping-net on a split bamboo cane. It was full of holes, but who cared? Fedora wasn't planning to catch shrimps. It was Tiddles she was after and a cat was bigger by design.

Sneaking out of the back door, while her mum was fielding an embarrassing phone call from a livid librarian (Fedora had been putting her own books on the library shelves and then trying to fine the library for not returning them on time), Fedora ran to the bottom of her garden and wriggled through a hole in the fence that opened out on to a small triangular piece of waste ground on the other side.

This was where the local feline population had a not-so-secret meeting place. From her bedroom window, she had often seen them, cats from all over, gathering to do whatever it was that cats liked to do; discuss the price of fish, or boast about the mice that got away, or just laze around in the sun licking their ears and flicking their tails at passing bumble bees.

Fedora was hoping to catch Tiddles here, engrossed in animated cat chat, but, sadly, the waste ground was empty. The shrimping-net drooped in her hand. She might have to wait days before Tiddles showed up. That was assuming Tiddles wasn't already dead, squashed into pussy purée by a ten ton truck with a sucker-footed Garfield on the windscreen.

Suddenly, there was a rustle in the bushes over to Fedora's right. She leapt behind a tree and held her breath, sneaking a furtive glance round the thick trunk when she thought it was safe to do so. A huge black tom-cat with a scratched nose and a torn ear paced across the grass, displaying his scars like a strutting general showing off his war medals. It was completely unaware of Fedora's presence, and this gave the bounty hunter a brilliant idea. Forget Tiddles! Any cat would do. After all they all looked pretty much the same. They all had four legs, whiskers and a tail. Besides, Angela Tearful sounded like a real cry-baby and if her eyes were as full of salty water as Fedora expected they might be, Angela wouldn't be able tell the difference between her precious little Tiddles and a manky old flea carpet!

Fedora waited until the tom-cat was asleep in the sun before pouncing on it with her shrimping-net. A basket of juicy rats' tails turned into dust as the cat's dream was shattered. It woke with a start and leapt three feet in the air, turning cartwheels in the net, tangling its paws and trapping its tail through the split in the bamboo pole. Fedora dropped to her knees and smothered the struggling cat with her body, until she had knocked the wind right out of it. Then she stood up and carried it down the road to Angela Tearful's house.

'Yes?' said Angela's mother as she opened the front door.

'I've brought Tiddles home,' lied Fedora. 'I've come for my reward.'

'Wait there,' said Angela's mum, calling up the stairs for Angela to come down quickly.

Angela was a tiny little girl with red blobby eyes and pale skin that clung to her cheek bones like wet sheets.

'Oh Tiddles!' she cried, as she ran across the hall with outstretched arms.

'You've brought my Tiddles back.' Fedora raised her hand.

'Money first,' she said, like a kidnapper collecting a ransom. 'Then you get the pussy cat.'

'Can't I see him first?' wept Angela, blowing her nose on the ten pound note. 'It might be the wrong cat.'

'Has Tiddles got a tail?' asked Fedora. 'And a rough tongue?' Angela nodded. 'Then, it's definitely her,' said the catty con-girl, holding out her hand for the filthy lucre.

But Angela's mother was not quite as stupid as her over-emotional daughter and *insisted* on seeing the cat first. When Fedora unfolded the dazed tom-cat from inside her coat, Angela made a noise like bath water slurping down a plug-hole. She gasped and grunted and shuddered and shook, and wept buckets of immature tears that gushed down the front path like a flooding river and puddled into a deep lake by the garden gate.

'Is there a problem?' enquired Fedora, innocently.

'That is not Tiddles,' said Angela's mother crossly. 'Tiddles is sort of marmaladey with white paws and a diamond-shaped brooch on her forehead.'

'Like a queen's tiara,' simpered Angela. Then she wailed for the whole street to hear, 'Oh, where are you Tiddles? Where is the Queen of the Pussy Cats?'

Fedora wanted to tell Angela to pull herself together, but the girl needed a shrink not home-truths from a stranger. So, instead, she said, 'Sorry to have troubled you,' and marched smartly back down the path with the perplexed pussy slung over her shoulder like a moth-eaten mink stole.

Well, by this time, Fedora's money glands were right up. There was ten pounds waiting for her in Angela's sweaty palms if only she could find the right cat, or at the very least match up the one she'd already got with the one Angela wanted.

She left the tom-cat on her father's work bench in the garage while she went inside to find the blurred photograph of Tiddles. When she returned, she had a tin of red boot-polish in one hand, a pastry shape-cutter in the other and a packet of flour in her pocket. She masked off the cat's tail with Sellotape to protect its natural blackness, then set about the poor tom, rubbing the boot-polish into its fur with a duster and buffing it up with a shoe-brush, until it shone like a bright red teapot.

Unfortunately, the result was not quite as marmaladey as Fedora would have liked; more crimsony with a hint of bright scarlet. It looked more like a fox with a black curly tail than a cat, but Fedora hadn't finished yet. She filled a baking-tray with flour, squirted the tom-cat's paws with lashings of wood glue and walked the bewildered beast through the flour bath. The red fox-tom-cat with a black curly tail now had four white paws, but still no marking on its forehead. For this, she used the pastry shape-cutter as a stencil. She strapped it just above the cat's eyes, and employed a small brush and a large amount of white emulsion to paint in the Queen of the Pussy Cat's diamond tiara. Then she stood back and admired her handiwork.

The tom-cat was a magnificent fake. Tiddles to a tee.

Whether it was the red boot polish smeared across Fedora's coat and hands, or the thin streak of white paint trickling down the tom-cat's nose, or the globs of sticky flour that were dripping on to the hall carpet, I don't know, but Angela and her mother took one look at Fedora's fake and shouted, 'That is *not* Tiddles!'

'It's close,' said Fedora. 'It must be worth a fiver, at least.'

'Go away,' ordered Angela's mother.

'Four quid?' The door was slammed in Fedora's face, causing the polished tom-cat to jump out of her arms and escape down the street, leaving a trail of red and white dough balls behind it.

Fedora realised she'd have to be twice as cunning to wangle the ten pound note off her opponent. She returned to the Tearfuls' house the following night with a white

Persian cat that she'd trapped in a tree by hanging sardines off its branches.

'I've got Tiddles,' she declared, presenting the white ball of fluff to Angela, who was distinctly third rate at dealing with disappointment.

'But Tiddles is marmalade,' she bawled.

'Was,' corrected Fedora. 'She was so shocked when she thought she'd lost you that her fur turned completely white.'

'No!' shouted Angela's mother.

'Right,' said Fedora.

An hour later, she was back at the door with a dog.

'Tiddles . . .' she declared, proudly.

'Is a cat,' whimpered Angela, dabbing her swollen eyes.

'. . . Is *inside* this dog,' continued the girl of a thousand lies. 'It ate her.' Angela's sobs could be heard in Billerickie, as her howling heart near-burst the buttons on her ruffled blouse.

'No!' roared Angela's mother.

'Right,' said Fedora.

Half an hour later, she returned with a tennis racket.

'Tiddles is home,' she said, 'and I claim my ten pounds!'

'Where?' yelped the much-gulled Angela Tearful, gullibly searching the empty path.

'In the frame,' explained Fedora, handing over the racket. 'The strings are cat gut, but it's definitely Tiddles. I checked the twang.'

'No!' boomed Angela's mother.

'Right,' said Fedora.

Ten minutes later, she was strolling up the path with a red pepperoni pizza in her hands.

'A pizza?' queried Angela, who couldn't remember ordering one.

'No, Tiddles,' clarified Fedora. 'Flattened by a passing car. Lovely with an olive on top.' Angela boo-hooed like an alpine horn and wrung her hands through an imaginary mangle.

'No!' shrieked Angela's mother.

'Right,' said Fedora. But this time she wasn't coming back. She had run out of ideas. Much as it pained her, she would just have to pass up Angela Tearful's measly ten pounds, and that was the end of that.

Fedora Funklefink was not used to defeat. It hung heavily round her shoulders like a dead stag, slowing her down to a shuffle as she made her way home. She was just crossing the road when a marmalade streak shot out in front of her and was hit by a car. There was a thump, then growing silence as the car disappeared into the distance. Fedora peered out into the middle of the road where the flattened lump lay steaming. She checked both ways before edging out to take a closer look.

It was a marmalade cat with a black tail and a diamond-shaped marking on its forehead. It was Tiddles, pancake-flat, but still dead useful! Scraping the squashed cat up off the tarmac, Fedora rushed it back to her dad's workshop where she inflated its body with a bicycle pump, put some colour back into its mouth with her mum's lipstick and tied a piece of invisible fishing line round the teeth of its lower jaw to make its mouth open and close.

'Not you again!' groaned Angela's mother, when Fedora rang on the doorbell a few minutes later.

'I really have found Tiddles this time,' said Fedora. 'Look,' and she produced the pumped up cat from underneath her coat, sat it across her left arm like a ventriloquist's dummy, and unwound its rigid black tail until it hung down stiffly like a clock's pendulum. 'She's pleased to be home, too,' she said, turning her head away and squeezing a secret miaow through her lips, whilst pulling on the fishing line that worked Tiddles's mouth.

'Look, she's saying she loves me,' beamed Angela Tearful, hearing her cat mew for the first time in three days. She clapped her little hands together and jumped up and down like a newborn lamb. 'Mummy it's Tiddles! She's come back to me!'

'And that's not all she's learnt while she's been away,' continued Fedora, warming to her trustful audience. 'She's learned how to talk as well.' Then she turned her head away for a second time and made the stiffening cat speak in a tongue that Angela could understand.

'Give Fedora Funklefink her ten pounds,' said Tiddles, miraculously. Angela and her mother gasped in amazement.

'No, actually give her twenty, gecause she found me and grought me home safely!' (Fedora was having trouble with her b's).

'Oh Fedora, thank you,' said Angela. 'I'm going to give you fifty pounds, because you've been so good to me.'

'Quite right too,' said Tiddles, and Fedora handed over the dead cat in exchange for a crisp new fifty pound note.

'It's been a pleasure doing business with you,' smirked Fedora. Then she ran off down the path, leaving Angela and her mother telling their Queen of the Pussy Cats that they were going to give her a nice warm bath, because she was smelling just a little bit yucky.

Fedora Funklefink danced down the street clasping the fifty pound note to her chest. It had been the cleverest scam she had ever turned. What a pair of dolts Angela and her mother were. Fancy not noticing that their precious pet was pushing up the daisies!

'They'll find out soon enough though,' she chortled, 'when they try to force its stiff little legs through the cat flap!'

She was laughing so much that she bumped into the tree where she had first found Angela's notice. Imagine her surprise, therefore, when what she saw in front of her nose was another piece of paper. Another reward. Another lost cat. Fedora could hardly believe her luck. She tore the notice off the bark and devoured its message greedily.

> ## LOST CAT
>
> Tigor is lost. Please help us to find him. He was last seen crossing the common and heading towards Sidcup. He has very distinctive markings Marmalade stripes with a black tail and a diamond patch right in the middle of his forehead.
> THERE IS A £5,000 REWARD FOR ANYONE WHO FINDS HIM!
>
> *Mario Bellasconi*

Five thousand pounds! FIVE THOUSAND POUNDS! Fedora would kill for five thousand pounds! This was one precious pussy cat. Her tongue drooled like a water slide as she imagined spending all that lovely dosh. After all, wasn't she the Cat–Catcher Supreme? Wasn't her shrimping–net feared throughout the feline world? Wasn't—

She heard something purr behind her! Fedora snickered. Tigor had come to her. This was easier than taking milk from a kitten. She'd have Tigor in the bag and the money in the bank before the day was out. She swivelled round, ready to pounce, and fixed her gaze on the pavement where she expected Tigor to be, but he was four feet higher up, with six inch teeth and a roar that shook the sky. Amber eyes, silky striped coat, paws like dustbin lids. Tigor took one look at Fedora and gobbled her up on the spot.

Tigor was a *big* cat. Tigor was a tiger. But Tigor got such bad tummyache from eating Fedora that he had to lie down on the pavement and go to sleep. Which is where the circus owner, Mario Bellasconi, found him.

So you see, Fedora Funklefink did capture Tigor and should have received the five thousand pound reward, but nobody knew where to find her.

Mr Peeler's Butterflies

Normally, night time is a peaceful affair, full of throat-throbbing snores and limp-lipped flutterings, full of snuggling and nuzzling and nestling and pillowy smells of sweet, wafting cork smoke and buttery toast. A time when the panting world breathes a sigh of relief and wraps itself up in the cool black silk of the night sky. A time to rest, a time to recharge, a time to cannelloni in your duvet. In short, night-time is for sleep.

Alexander, however, thought differently. He was ten years old and wouldn't go to bed when his parents sent him.

'Can't I just see the end of this programme?' he whined.

It was already nine-thirty, two hours past his bedtime.

'No,' said his mother, firmly, and his father agreed.

'Absolutely, one hundred and ten per cent no!'

'But it's really, really good.'

'Alexander, it's the weather report!' wailed his mother. 'Since when have you had even the slightest interest in the weather?'

'Since you told him to go to bed,' muttered Alexander's father.

'It's educational,' squirmed the boy, rolling across the floor and wedging himself underneath the coffee-table, so that his parents couldn't grab him. 'I'm learning about isobars and warm fronts.'

'I'll give you a warm behind in a minute,' threatened his father, rising from the sofa.

'Oh please, please, please!' begged the burrowing boy. 'Just five minutes more!' His father grabbed his ankles and dragged him out into the middle of the sitting-room floor.

'BED!' he blasted. 'NOW!'

'Will you carry me?' asked Alexander, knowing full well that this would add precious seconds to the climb upstairs.

'If you promise to go to sleep when you get into bed,' sighed his mother wearily, sagging under the weight of her son as he leapt into her arms and stuck his thumb in his mouth.

'I'm not tired, you know,' he said.

'Yes, well, we are!' glowered his father. 'Goodnight!'

And with that, he collapsed back on to the sofa and went straight to sleep.

Alexander made his mother stop on the landing outside his bedroom.

'Just checking the cat's not up here,' he said, scanning the floor. 'Don't want her sleeping on my face, do I? OK, proceed.' His mother dumped him on to his bed.

'Good night,' she panted.

'Good night,' said Alexander, pretending to climb under his duvet. 'Whoops! I've forgotten to brush my teeth. Don't go away now, will you?' And he scooted into the bathroom before his mother could nail him. She sank to her knees and rested her tired head on the bed. The crumpled duvet smothered her ears and its warm folds tugged at her eyelids. 'Back again!' shouted Alexander, racing into the room and diving across the bed, like he was scoring England's winning try at Twickenham.

'Good,' she said blearily. 'Now perhaps we can all get some sleep.'

'Not until I've put my shiny swimming costume on,' bounced the small boy.

'Your what?' said his mother in astonishment.

'Oh, I always wear it over my pyjamas,' he informed her, rushing over to the chest of drawers in the corner. 'The sparkle keeps the Bogey Man away.' Alexander's mother didn't have the foggiest idea what he was talking about. 'The Bogey Man hates the sparkly bits when they shine in his eyes,' he explained slowly, like his mother had the brains of a junked jelly baby. Then he pulled his rainbow-coloured trunks over his pyjama trousers and adopted a Mr Universe, bicep-flexing pose in front of his mirror. 'Looking good!' he growled at himself.

'Are you ready now?' yawned his mother.

'Yes,' announced Alexander, cartwheeling into bed. 'Ready for beddy!' but, of course he wasn't. He was still just warming up. He could keep his bedtime delaying tactics going all night, if necessary. 'Have you checked the curtains?' he asked.

'Yes, they're closed,' replied his mother.

'No, but *really* closed? I mean so tight that I can't see any light coming through them at all. Could you do them again, please?' His mother rose from the bed and overlapped the edges of the curtains.

'Satisfied?' she enquired.

'Lovely!' said Alexander. 'Now my light.'

'But I've just closed the curtains,' snapped his mother. 'Why do you need a light on?'

'Different sorts of light,' giggled Alexander under his duvet. If he was good, he could spin this explanation out for at least five minutes. 'You see, one's a sort of outside light, you know, outside—'

'Yes I know, outside,' said his mother.

'And that one's all cold and moony, but the other – that's the inside light, obviously – well, the other's all warm

19

and cosy like sucking on a strong cough sweet.' His mother raised her hand sharply to call a halt to her scheming son's wittering.

'I'll do it,' she said, switching on his bedside light, kissing him on the forehead and turning to leave the room. Alexander waited until she was on the landing before shouting.

'Toys, Mummy!'

'Not tonight,' she implored him, in a high, squeaky voice. 'Go to sleep Alexander.'

'But I can't sleep unless I've got all my toys in bed with me,' he cried, turning on the water works, to make his need appear that much more desperate.

'Which ones?' demanded his mother crossly, re-entering the room like a stomping majorette. Alexander's manipulative face exploded into a sunny smile.

'I want Flopsy and Mopsy,' he said, pointing to the two rabbits that he had been given on his first birthday, 'my Action Man, that fire-engine over there on the top shelf, those framed Ace of Base pictures on the wall, my rubber dinosaur, Billy . . .' As he reeled off his list, his mother flew around the room collecting the toys. She flung back the duvet, piled them on to Alexander's legs and pulled the duvet back up.

'There!' she said. 'Happy now?'

'And the wind-up mouse in my shoe,' whispered Alexander, innocently.

'And where's your shoe?'

'Downstairs,' he said, trying to smother his sniggering.

'Alexander, please,' begged his mother.

'I shall cry!'

'Wait here.' His mother stormed out of the room and stamped down the stairs, returning a couple of minutes later empty handed. 'There was no wind-up mouse in your shoe,' she seethed.

'I know, I just found it in my hand,' apologised Alexander. 'Sorry. It must have been there all the time.' His mother's eyes were twitching. Her mouth was sharp and humourless. 'Are you going to read me a story?'

'No!'

'Could I have my tape on then?'

'GO TO SLEEP!' she roared, wailing out of the room like a wonky police siren. Alexander turned to face the curtains and smiled. He'd give her seven minutes, just enough time to get settled downstairs.

It was now ten thirty.

'Oh, Mummy!' came the little voice from the top of the stairs. 'Oh, Daddy!'

'What do you want now?' came the plaintive call from below.

'I can't sleep.'

'Well try shutting your eyes,' bawled his livid father.

'But the landing light's not on and I'm scared,' whimpered

Alexander, scuttling into the bathroom to splash fake tap tears on to his cheeks. Then he huddled pathetically by the banisters and waited for his father to emerge from the sitting-room. Sure enough, seconds later, his heavy step pounded up the stairs.

'You are a thorough nuisance,' he hissed, switching on the landing light. 'There.'

'I'm thirsty,' pleaded Alexander. 'I need a drink of water.'

'Right!' His father got him one, spilling most of the glass over the carpet in his fury and haste. 'Now will you go to bed?'

'Can I go to the loo first?'

'Why?' exclaimed his father. Alexander snorted.

'It's that glass of water,' he said. His father tapped his foot on the landing carpet while Alexander went into the bathroom and pretended to pee. 'Aaaahhh, yes!' sighed the boy, loudly, behind the door, 'that's much better.' Then he pulled the chain and padded back into his bedroom.

'Anything else?' enquired his father, sarcastically. 'If you keep this up much longer, Alexander, it'll be morning and you won't need to go to bed at all!'

'I learned how to do a handstand today,' said the boy, cheekily. 'Do you want to see it?' His father's raised hand said no. 'Only joking,' said Alexander. 'I feel sleepy now.'

'Then, goodnight,' said his father, emphatically. 'And if either of us have to come up again, I promise you'll regret it.'

Alexander held his breath until his father was halfway down the stairs. Then he cried out, 'Daddy!' in his loudest voice. The door nearly burst off its hinges as his father steamed back into the room.

'WHAT IS IT NOW?' he bellowed.

'Goodnight,' whispered Alexander, snuggling down into his duvet and closing his eyes. 'Honestly, you grown-ups, you're such cross-patches!'

It was eleven-thirty.

Once his father had shut the sitting-room door, Alexander sat up in bed and played with his Game Boy for an hour until his parents went to bed. As they shuffled past his door, like a couple of crumbly old snails, he pretended to be fast asleep, whilst secretly watching them out of the corner of his eye.

What pathetically weary creatures they are, he thought to himself. *Needing sleep! Huh! I ask you.*

What Alexander failed to understand was that he too needed sleep, for in the mornings he was the grumpiest, thumpiest, clumpiest child in the world. But he thought he was different. He thought that going to sleep was a cissy thing to do, and besides, where was the fun in doing what his boring old parents asked?

It was four o'clock in the morning. Alexander had only been asleep for ten minutes, when the latch on his window slid across with a sharp click. He turned over in his bed, snuffled like a contented piglet, and scratched his nose. But he didn't wake up. The sash-window jarred in its runners as it juddered open and a fishy smell wafted into Alexander's bedroom, followed by a single pink butterfly with combed, black wings. It fluttered into the middle of the room and settled on the foot of Alexander's bed as a light footfall dropped on to the carpet behind the curtains.

Alexander woke with a start.

'Who's there?' he cried. There was no reply. 'Mummy! Daddy!' He rubbed his eyes and peered through the gloom at his empty room.

'What is it?' shouted his mother, stumbling across the landing.

'There's something in my bedroom,' blinked Alexander. 'I heard it come in.'

The butterfly flew silently to the top of Alexander's wardrobe and hid in the shadows.

'What is going on now?' roared Alexander's father, as he barged into the room wearing a large pair of white underpants. 'I warned you Alexander!'

'I was woken up, honest I was. There's something in here.'

'Nonsense,' growled his father, flicking a switch and groaning as the light exploded in the back of his eyes. 'I'm fed up with your games. The room is empty.'

'But I can smell fish,' persisted Alexander.

'He's right,' said his mother. 'It smells like sardines.'

'Socks more likely,' grumbled Alexander's father,

checking to see that the window was closed, which it was.
'There,' he barked. 'Satisfied?'

'But I heard something drop to the floor.'

'Probably this,' said his father, bending down to pick
up a small metal tin that was lying on its side against the
skirting-board. He held it up to the light. 'It's a tin of
sardines,' he said, baffled by his discovery.

'Well, I didn't put it there,' protested Alexander.

'Then who did?' shouted his father. 'Mr Peeler?'

'Mr who?' asked his wife.

'At least, it explains the smell of fish,' he croaked. 'Now
can we all please go back to sleep. I've had enough of your
antics to last me a lifetime, Alexander.'

'Mr who?' repeated his wife.

'What?'

'That name you just mentioned.'

'Oh, Peeler. You must know it. That Victorian nursery
rhyme:

> "Sleep, sleep, now close your eyes,
> Don't tempt our Mr Peeler.
> For if you lie awake at night,
> You'll summon the sleep-stealer." '

Alexander's mouth had dropped open like an oven door.

'What does sleep-stealer mean?' he gasped.

'How should I know?' exploded his father. 'It's a nursery

rhyme like Jack and Jill. It doesn't mean anything.' But Alexander didn't like the sound of this Mr Peeler, real or not. 'I'm back to bed,' moaned his father. 'Some of us need our sleep.' And he staggered out, misjudging where the door was and cracking his head on the wall.

Alexander looked at his mother who was swaying on her feet.

'I don't think I can sleep now,' he said, quietly.

'So what's new?' yawned his mother. 'I'll see you in the morning and please don't wake us up with any more of your tricks.' Then she too was gone, leaving Alexander all alone in his bedroom with the light still on.

The pink-skinned butterfly fluttered down from its perch on the wardrobe. Alexander rubbed his eyes and peered at the strange insect as it landed on his duvet. When it flapped its wings, it looked like it was blinking.

'Sleep, sleep, now close your eyes,' whispered the soft, echoing voice in Alexander's ear. 'Don't tempt our Mr Peeler.'

The boy spun round, but the voice jumped across the room as quick as a silverfish.

'For if you lie awake at night . . .' Alexander froze. '. . . You'll summon the sleep-stealer.'

A small fat man had appeared at the end of Alexander's bed. He was wearing a yellow chequered waistcoat and baggy tweed trousers tucked into his boots. His face was round and ruddy with mutton-chop sideburns that swept off his cheeks and covered his winged collar and neckerchief. A thousand butterflies hovered above his head, like a shimmering, floating crown, and in his hand he held a small butterfly net and a silver bodkin-like key.

'Still not asleep?' he rasped, invading the room with his sardine breath. Alexander wanted to scream, but his tongue had set fast in his mouth. He shook his head.

'I want you to know that I'm wearing my sparkly swimming trunks, so you can't hurt me,' he blustered, falteringly. The man broke into peals of laughter that sounded like they echoed from the white-button end of a long tunnel. 'I know who you are,' shuddered Alexander.

'And I know who you is, too,' said the jovial fish-guzzler. 'So isn't that nice? Sort of cosy, like.'

'You're Mr Peeler.'

'Have been now for near two hundred years, so guess I still am,' said Mr Peeler. 'And you's Alexander.'

'I'm going to scream,' said the boy as Mr Peeler took a glide towards him.

'Go ahead,' smiled the intruder. 'But you's fair tuckered your mother and father out. They wouldn't wake up tonight if the whole street came bashing down the door. Besides, if they did, they'd just think it was another one of your silly games to put off sleeping.' He was standing right beside Alexander's bed now, leering at him with his rotten teeth.

'What do you want?' said the boy, retreating under his duvet.

'I want you to keep your eyes open for Mr Peeler,' said the grizzled man, winking at Alexander with one of his large, pop-out peepers.

'But you're already here,' said the quivering wreck of a boy.

'That's not quite what I meant,' said his visitor, laying the butterfly net down on the bed and patting Alexander's cheek. 'You see it occurs to me that them boys and girls what don't want to go to sleep, can't be doing it just to upset their mothers and fathers. No, I reckons they does it, 'cause they likes it! Which is sort of where I come in. I'm here to help!' He flashed out the silver key from behind his back. 'Ever rolled back a sardine tin lid with one of these, Alexander?' But Alexander was not listening.

'You can't steal my sleep,' he shouted. 'It's mine. I need it!' He was struggling to escape the fat man's grasp.

'Bit late for a change of heart now, boy,' brayed Mr Peeler. 'You want to stay awake all night and I's here to make sure you do!' And with one quick movement he reached forward with the key and peeled Alexander's eyelids clean off his face.

Alexander stared, unblinkingly, out into the room. Mr Peeler was catching the butterflies in his net and sticking them on to his eyelids. Their fluttering wings made his eyelashes ten feet long, and, as they fluttered, he rose from the ground and flew across to the window.

'You see,' said Mr Peeler, 'these aren't butterflies at all, just all them blinking eyelids what I've peeled off all you blinking kids.' He sat Alexander's eyelids on top of the butterfly pile and unfastened the window catch. 'Now you see me and now you see me again!' he quipped, 'and again and again and again!' Then he flew into the night sky, with his voice trailing off like a shooting-star. 'Keep your eyeballs peeled for Mr Peeler!'

Alexander never slept again. No matter how tired he became he couldn't close his eyes, which made him wish (rather a lot in fact) that he'd just gone to sleep when his parents had told him to.

Night night. Sleep tight.

Fat Boy with a Trumpet
A True Story

Johnny Bullneck was a bully. If he came up to you in the playground and asked who your favourite football team was you had to say Millwall, else he'd twist your arm up your back and dead leg you. He never brought his own rulers or pencils or rubbers into school, because there were always sixty smaller boys who'd hand him theirs without being asked twice. And if he was hungry he just went through your pockets for sweets, while his gang pinned your arms to your side and tweaked your ears like they were podding peas from a shell.

'Here, Miles.'

'Who, me?'

'Yes, you. There's nobody else as ugly, is there?' Collapse of gang into hysterics. 'I want a tin of spotted paint. Get me some.'

'*Spotted* paint, you say?'

'It must be red spots.'

'Red spotted paint, right.'

'Three gallons by lunch time, all right?'

'Three gallons of red spotted paint by lunch-time. Should be OK, yeah.' Gang now busting their trouser buttons with sycophantic giggling.

'And a left handed screwdriver . . .'

Miles sneaked out of school before lunch and was never seen again. Rumour has it he couldn't find the paint and the screwdriver, so didn't dare come back. He made his parents move up North, to Darlington, where he started at a new school under an assumed name. Sheila Gish was what we heard.

Johnny was huge, awkward and twelve years old. Short-haired, flat-footed, white-fleshed and pudgy, because he snatched everyone else's food at lunch and never left the table before he'd guzzled at least twelve helpings. He hated fat people though, which was really weird because he was one himself. Someone once said that he came from a broken home, but if he did it was only because *he'd* broken it. He never smiled. It was like he was born sneering, like he came out of his mum complaining to the doctor that the light was too bright and he'd bash the doctor if he didn't dim it. And because he never smiled, none of us knew if we were doing right by him or simply getting him more annoyed. Let's face it, the only time you knew where you stood with Johnny Bullneck was when he was duffing you up. He was a head case, he was dangerous to know, and he always wanted whatever it was you'd got.

With grown-ups though, Johnny Bullneck was a coward. If a teacher shouted at him, or the lollipop lady outside our school scolded him for running into the road, he'd burst into tears. It seemed like he was King of the World when he was the biggest, but all mouth and no trousers when the tables were reversed.

We all hated him, of course, but only in secret. It wouldn't have done the shape of our noses much good to tell him to his face. We hated him for the way he couldn't see beyond a person's size or the way they looked. We hated him for giving us big yellow bruises that hurt when you pressed them and for being a jerk and for turning every sunny day into a thunder-storm.

One day a new boy joined our class. Timothy his name was. A shy bloke with little, round, metal-framed glasses, who looked at his shoes all day and spoke to the teacher through the top of his head. He was different though. He was huge, big bones he said, and he played the trumpet. Boy, could he play the trumpet. He did 'Yankee Doodle Went To Town' for us in the playground and it sounded just like it had come off a record. Anyway, Johnny took one look at this new boy and earmarked him for grief. It was partly because Timothy was fat, but mainly because he was new and Johnny had to teach him who was boss.

It was at first break that Johnny trapped Timothy round the back of the cricket pavilion (actually it was a small garden hut where the groundsman made his tea, but the headmaster said it was better for the school's image if we called it a pavilion) and asked him if he'd brought his photo with him.

'What photo?' mumbled Timothy.

'Your medical photo,' said Johnny with a cocky shake of his head that signalled a spontaneous chorus of 'Yeah, your medical photo,' from his gang.

'No,' said Timothy. 'Nobody told me.'

'Nobody told you?' mimicked Johnny. 'That's terrible, because, you see, by law if you don't have one on your first day they expel you.'

'Really?' Timothy was curled up against the back wall of the shed, protecting himself from he didn't know what.

'I'll do you a favour,' said Johnny, 'because I can see that you and me are going to be friends. I've got a camera with me. I'll take your photo now, save you getting into trouble later.' Timothy shook his head, meaning no thanks, but Johnny wasn't trying to be nice. 'Take your clothes off and stand over there on the cricket pitch,' he said. And when Timothy didn't move he said it again, only this time he stepped right up close and whispered it in Timothy's

33

ear, and didn't step back until Timothy had done as he was told.

He was huddled there, clutching his trumpet case, all plumply pink and goosebumped like a plucked turkey, while Johnny's gang roared with laughter and pointed at his stomach. Then Johnny looked at his camera and said, 'Whoops, I seem to have forgotten to put a film in!' just as the school bell rang.

The gang ran off, but not before Johnny had thrown Timothy's clothes up on to the roof of the shed, so that when the headmaster looked out of his window to check that everyone was in from break, he got the shock of his life.

Timothy got five hundred lines:

I must not remove my clothes on top of the cricket pavilion again. It is an unpleasant sight that distracts other pupils from their academic pursuits.

The medical photo prank was just Johnny's way of warming up. At lunch-time, he pushed all the other kids off Timothy's table so that he and his gang could sit next to him.

'You should be on a diet,' he said, stealing two potatoes off Timothy's plate. 'A great big tub of lard like you doesn't want to be eating food. Slimming pills is what you need, or a dose of this.' Johnny put a bar of chocolate down on the table. 'Go on, eat it. It's lovely.'

'It's a laxative,' muttered Timothy.

'It's chocolate, you bozo. I thought fat boys liked chocolate.'

'It'll make me ill.'

'It'll make you thin,' sneered Johnny, poking Timothy with a fork. 'Now come along, baby, eat it all up like Mummy says.' The gang gagged with glee at Johnny's joke and spluttered their lunch all over their plates. Timothy was forced to eat the entire bar and then to lick the silver wrapper clean.

The laxative took a grip on Timothy's belly right in the middle of double maths. He screamed out of the room with a face as red as a baboon's bum and didn't come back for a week.

When he did, Johnny was waiting for him. He grabbed Timothy's glasses as he walked through the school gates and put them on.

'Guess who I am?' he said, puffing out his cheeks and walking round stiff-limbed like the Michelin man. The gang was in stitches as Johnny lay on his back and kicked his legs in the air. 'Help! I can't get up,' he cried, playing the stranded turtle.

Timothy was crying. 'Give them back,' he said. 'I can't see a thing without my glasses.'

Johnny jumped to his feet. 'Oh, is the little baby all upset?' he mocked. 'Is little baby as blind as a bat without his spectacles? Come and get them then, Specky. If you can find them that is!' Then Johnny ran off to the other side of the playground while the gang shoved Timothy after him. But Timothy couldn't see where he was going and the gang kept tripping him up, so that he skidded over the concrete and cut his knees and elbows to shreds. 'Don't let go of your trumpet will you, Four-eyes?' taunted Johnny, as he dangled the glasses just out of Timothy's reach. 'What's it like down there in the dark?'

The rest of us boys should have gone in to help, but you know what it's like when you're scared. No one wants to become the next victim. It took a girl called Tina to stop Johnny's vicious game. She went right up to him and shouted in his face.

'You're a horrible brute!' she hollered. 'What harm's he ever done to you? Give him his glasses back!' This gave Johnny a new line of attack. 'You great, fat wimp,' he snarled at Timothy, who was curled up on the ground at Johnny's feet. 'Got to get a girl to do your fighting for you now. You pathetic porky. I could smash your glasses right now and there's nothing you could do about it!'

But Tina was a girl of action as well as of words and she snatched the glasses out of Johnny's hands before he could carry out his threat.

'Why don't you grow up, Johnny Bullneck,' she said, and all the other girls clapped her. You could see that Johnny was furious. He was breathing heavily and his mouth had tightened like a punctured rubber ring. Tina had just made him look weak in front of the rest of the school and he had to do something quick to recover his power base.

'Right,' he shouted, 'if I can't have your glasses, then I'll have your trumpet instead!'

But as he grabbed Timothy's trumpet case and gave it an almighty heave, something extraordinary happened. Timothy found a huge voice from deep in his boots that had us all reeling from shock. He stood up and bellowed, 'NO, YOU CAN'T HAVE MY TRUMPET!' and snatched it back.

Johnny turned white, whether with fear or fury none of us knew, but he let go of the case just the same. Then they just stood there, squared off like two gunfighters, and Timothy looked about twelve feet tall, while Johnny looked like a midget.

I guess it was then that we knew that Johnny had met his match, that some day soon he'd get what was coming to him, but never in a million years could we have guessed how it would finally happen.

It was a week later. Johnny had been brooding for days, like a fighting dog on a short leash, plotting his cowardly revenge on Timothy. He got his chance after school one Friday night. Timothy used to walk home across the common along the path behind the school cricket nets. Johnny and his mates had been given permission to use the nets after school by Sergeant, the groundsman. At four o'clock, Johnny went to the pavilion to get a cricket bat and six balls.

'What's with the sudden interest in cricket, Bullneck?' asked Sergeant, as he rummaged around in the cricket bag for a set of stumps. 'I've never seen you play before.'

'Got to start some time,' said Johnny. 'Who knows, I might be the answer to England's prayers.'

'A likely story,' replied Sergeant. 'There's a storm brewing out there. If it starts to rain, I want this equipment under cover sharpish, you understand? You leave it out over the weekend and I'll have your guts for garters.' Johnny nodded, but he wasn't listening. He was slipping the length of rope that Sergeant used to mark out the batting crease into his blazer pocket.

Outside, the sky was black. Thunder clouds rolled overhead like iodined cotton-wool. Johnny and his gang made their way over to the nets as the first drops of rain exploded on their skin, warm and heavy. A clap of thunder rumbled in the distance as they set up the stumps, before hiding behind the big tree on the path, from where they would spring their ambush.

Timothy left the school building with his trumpet tucked safely underneath his arm. The last week had been better since Johnny had stopped picking on him. He walked past the cricket pavilion, along the path in front of the sixth-form centre and struck out across the playing-fields towards the common. The rain was falling more heavily as he drew level with the nets. He noticed the stumps set up for a game that nobody was playing, but he was getting soaked and didn't stop to wonder why. The clouds clashed above his head with a shattering boom as he reached the path. The trees acted like a huge umbrella and he slowed down, savouring the dry musty smell that steamed off the leaves.

Suddenly, the air was filled with shouting and shadowy figures fell on him from all sides. They grabbed him, knocking his trumpet to the ground. A hand snatched off his glasses, tearing the metal springs from behind his ears. He was caught like a bear in a trap, outnumbered and overpowered. His hands were tied behind his back and his ankles hobbled with Sergeant's rope. He was rolled through the mud and dragged to his feet in front of the stumps at the far end of the net.

'You're going to regret you ever crossed swords with me,' spat Johnny Bullneck. Timothy was petrified.

'I need my glasses,' he said.

'Oh, but you can't bat in glasses, Timothy. Think how dangerous it would be if a ball smashed into your eye. Don't worry, I'll wear them for safe keeping.' Johnny was playing it dead cool, toying with his victim like all bullies do when they've got the upper hand.

'Where's my trumpet?'

'Safe as houses,' said Johnny, putting the brass instrument in his right hand. A streak of lightning lit up the sky over the common, as the rain pin-pricked Timothy's frightened face. 'Now, here's what we're going to do. We're going to bowl at you, Timothy.'

'But I need a bat and pads and gloves . . .'

'Why?'

'Or the balls will hit me!' quaked Timothy.

'I sincerely hope so,' taunted Johnny. 'That's why I've gone to the trouble of tying you up.' The thunder crashed above their heads like canons of war and drove the rain down like bullets from a gatling-gun. 'Have fun, my son. Duck and weave,' laughed Johnny, walking back up the net to the bowling end. Timothy slipped on the muddy ground as he tried to push his way out through the netting. 'Oh by the way,' called Johnny, 'I thought I'd play you a little tune on the trumpet while my friends are bowling. Any requests?'

'Don't do this!' wailed Timothy. 'Please!'

'Don't know that one,' snickered Johnny, much to his gang's amusement. 'I thought I'd do "I Don't Like Cricket", if it's all the same to you!' And with that Johnny gave the signal to his bowlers to start bowling whilst he put the trumpet to his lips to start trumpeting.

There was a crack of thunder from the sky and a shaft of lightning arrowed down towards the brass conductor. There was a blue flash, a puff of smoke and Johnny Bullneck's shrill squeak of surprise.

When Timothy dared to look up, rain had stopped play without a single ball being bowled. He could just make out the hazy figures of Johnny's gang as they ran screaming across the playing-fields towards the school. At the end of the net lay the frizzy-haired figure of Johnny Bullneck, smouldering gently like a day-old bonfire. In his hands, a blackened trumpet, around his eyes, two crimson rings where Timothy's glasses had burnt into his flesh.

And that's how Johnny Bullneck got fried. The lightning had shot straight down the trumpet and looped the loop round Timothy's metal-framed glasses. I remember the headmaster telling us all about it at assembly on Monday morning, but I don't recall a single person crying. Well, it's not as if it was a particularly painful way to go, was it? I mean, it *was* all over in a flash.

More's the pity.

and lashings of ginger beer!

The Chipper Chums Go Scrumping

What a summer hols it was! Algie and his best chum Col
(and Algie's dog Stinker) were spending six whizzing weeks
in Kent with Col's Aunt Fanny and Uncle Herbert. They
had made oodles of new friends during their stay and had
formed a ripping gang called The Chipper Chums for the
express purpose of having adventures. There was tousle-
haired Ginger and his little sister Alice, whose father was a
sea captain and captured pirates in the Indian Ocean, and
Sam, who lived in Honeysuckle Cottage at the end of
Sunnymeadow Lane. Sam was a girl with a boy's name,
but nobody teased her about it, because she was so big.
That horrible Dick Stick dared to once. He called Sam,

'Sam the man,' but Sam was the world's best boxer and simply beat Dick up. How they laughed, to see Dick sent packing with a bloody nose and tears streaming down his unwashed face.

'And jolly well don't come back,' shouted Sam, as Dick sneaked back to his mother, who was hanging out rat skins on the washing-line. The Sticks were so poor that they didn't have two pork chops to rub together, but what did the chums care, so long as the sun blazed down all day and the ginger beer flowed like wine!

One day, Algie and Col got out of bed.

'What a corker of a morning,' said Algie, enthusiastically, pulling back the curtains and looking out at the sunshine.

'It's a perfectly gorgeous day for a picnic,' agreed Col, pulling on his shorts and knee-length socks. 'I say, do you think Ginger, Alice and Sam would like to come with us? We could have an adventure.'

'Count me in,' cried Algie, as the bedroom door flew open and Stinker rushed in to join them. Stinker was a mixed up dog (Algie called him a Heinz 57, because he was fifty-seven different varieties!) with a long shaggy face and a tail that never stopped wagging. He leapt at Col and knocked him flat on the bed. Algie laughed as Stinker licked Col all over with his rough tongue and barked playfully.

'Yes, all right,' said Algie, patting his dog on the head, 'you can come too, old boy!' Stinker was so pleased that he jumped all over Algie and licked him too!

'I think we'd better go down for breakfast,' said Col. 'I can smell Aunt Fanny cooking muffins, kippers, kidneys and kedgeree in the kitchen.'

'Hoorah!' cheered the two boys. 'Kedgeree! Our favourite!' Then they pulled on their clothes and skipped downstairs with Stinker bounding along behind them.

'I think a picnic would be a very nice idea,' said Aunt Fanny as she took a loaf of freshly baked bread out of the oven. 'I've got some scones you could take and Uncle Herbert could pick some lovely tomatoes from the garden.' Uncle Herbert scratched his long beard.

'And maybe I could find some ginger beer in the cellar,' he said.

'Oh, would you Uncle Herbert!' shouted Algie and Col together. 'Ginger beer would be grand. And some home-made biscuits.'

'And thick slices of farmhouse cheddar cheese and lashings of fresh strawberries and cream,' added Algie. Aunt Fanny and Uncle Herbert laughed.

'Whoa there, you sly fellows!' joshed Uncle Herbert. 'We're not made of money. I'm not the King of England, you know!'

'Don't be so mean,' said Aunt Fanny. 'They're growing boys. They need all the food they can get. Now you two run along and play, while I prepare the hamper.'

'Gosh, thanks,' said Col, giving his aunt a kiss on the cheek. 'You're the best aunt a lad could wish for!' Then the boys ran out into the garden, leaving Aunt Fanny to prepare their slap-up picnic and wash up their plates from breakfast.

It was scorching hot outside, as Algie and Col cycled down the lane to Ginger's house.

'Can Ginger and Alice come out to play?' Col asked Ginger's mother, who was baking gingerbread men in the kitchen.

'We're having a picnic,' added Algie.

'Get down, Stinker,' said Ginger's mother, sternly. Stinker was trying to chew the legs off the gingerbread men.

'Gosh, I am sorry,' said Col. 'That's the trouble with dogs. They've got no manners.'

'Dogs will be dogs,' smiled Ginger's mother. 'It's good to see someone with an appetite round here. Now, you have a glass of my freshly squeezed lemonade while I go upstairs and see if Ginger and Alice are ready.' Two minutes later, Ginger and Alice came tumbling into the kitchen.

'Hoorah!' shouted Ginger. 'Am I glad to see you two. A picnic, you say?'

'And an adventure,' said Algie.

'Hoorah!' cheered Ginger again. 'Adventures are grand!'

'Can I bring my teddy-bear?' asked Alice, who was only three.

'Of course,' replied Col, 'the more the merrier, Alice. Besides if you need to have a sleep later on, you'll have something to cuddle!' Alice beamed from ear to ear. How she admired Col. He was always so nice to her.

'Now you'd better take some gingerbread men with you,' said Ginger's mother, 'just in case you get hungry before the picnic.'

'Ooh rather,' grinned Ginger. 'I simply love gingerbread men.' In fact, they all did, so Ginger's mother wrapped up a dozen in a muslin cloth and tucked them inside Ginger's blazer.

'Make sure you're back before sundown,' she waved, as they cycled off down the road towards Honeysuckle Cottage. 'And don't get into mischief!'

Sam was in the back garden, catapulting pebbles at a row of rusty tin-cans on top of the wooden fence.

'Morning men,' she roared.

'And girls,' said Alice sweetly.

'And Alice,' added Sam. 'How could I possibly forget you?' Alice grinned again. *Everyone* was so nice to her. Secretly she liked Sam more than all the others, though, because she was a big strong girl. 'What's the plan for today then?'

'We're going on a picnic,' said Algie. 'We'd love it awfully if you'd come too.'

'Just try to stop me,' bellowed Sam, twanging the braces on her thick corduroy trousers. 'There's nothing I like more on a hot day than a picnic with friends.' And they all cheered in agreement.

'Did I hear the word "picnic"?' came the voice of Sam's mother from the kitchen. 'I've just baked a cake. I'll put it in a tin and you can take it with you.'

'A cake!' gasped the chums, who could barely believe their luck. 'Yes please!'

'It's a Victoria sponge,' said Sam's mother, which made it just about as perfect a cake as any of them could think of.

Half an hour later, The Chipper Chums set off down the country lanes on their bikes. Col had the picnic hamper strapped to his rear mud-guard with string and Stinker bounded alongside them, barking at the trees and rushing into fields to chase startled rabbits. It was a fine day to be cycling and they swept past the hedgerows singing sunny songs at the tops of their excited voices.

> When you're in The Chipper Chums
> It sure banishes the glums,
> With the wind in our hair,
> Not a problem, not a care,
> And a picnic in our tums!

It was such jolly good fun that they didn't notice when Alice got left behind.

'I say, wait for me,' she shouted, as she watched the older boys and girls disappear round a corner. 'I can't keep up on my tricycle.' It was Ginger who stopped.

'Gosh, my little sister,' he said. 'I hope we haven't lost her.'

'I vote we stop,' said Sam, who as the biggest was also the most sensible. So they all stopped and waited for Alice to catch them up.

'Sorry, old thing,' apologised Ginger to his little sister. 'I feel a proper bounder. We promise not to cycle so fast again.'

'That's all right,' said Alice. 'It was Teddy who was scared!' Then they all laughed and everything was all right again.

They cycled across Buttercup Meadow and down through the wood to the stream that bubbled merrily alongside the apple orchard. The sun was so hot that they decided to get off their bikes and have their picnic there and then.

'But it's only eleven o'clock,' said Algie.

'Blow the time,' said Sam. 'I vote we eat if we're hungry.'

'Hear, hear,' agreed Ginger. 'I'm famished. Shall we start with the gingerbread men?'

'No, let's see what Aunt Fanny's put in the hamper first,' said Col. This was a jolly good idea and they all sat down on the grass, while Stinker plunged his muzzle into the stream and had a long refreshing drink of water.

'Poor thing, he must be ever so hot in all that fur,' said Alice.

'Well I prefer ginger beer!' said Algie, tugging open the

lid of the picnic hamper. 'I say, Col, look at the tuck your Aunt Fanny has prepared!'

It was a banquet fit for a prince. Sardine sandwiches, clotted cream scones, ripe, red tomatoes and a tin of spam. There was even a bone for Stinker. They all agreed that they had never seen such a sumptuous spread before. Sam found knives and forks and plates, while Algie opened two bottles of ginger beer and set them down on the grass. It was simply gorgeous.

Ten minutes later, Ginger lay back in the sun, feeling that he really couldn't eat any more. In fact they were all so full of good things that one by one they fell asleep in the warm grass. Stinker eyed them in astonishment. What sort of time was this for children to go to bed! But as he couldn't rouse them, he decided to join them and, resting his head over Col's legs, he closed his eyes and went to sleep.

When they woke up, the sun had gone behind a cloud and there was a chill in the air.

'I say, chaps,' said Sam, 'we'd better be getting home. It'll be dark soon.'

'But we haven't had our adventure yet,' moaned Algie. 'What shall we do?'

'How about fishing?' suggested Col. 'I've got some string in my pocket. If we find a stick we can make a rod and use one of Alice's hair grips to make a hook.'

'I don't wear hair grips,' said Alice.

'We could pull out one of Teddy's eyes,' said Ginger,

'and bend the pin on the back of that.' But it was a frightfully cruel thing to say and Alice started crying.

'That was not a nice thing to say to poor Alice. She loves Teddy,' said Sam, putting her arms round Alice's shoulders.

'Oh I say, I'm most awfully sorry, old girl. I forgot that Teddy was yours,' said Ginger, who felt like a total cad. 'Perhaps you'd like to choose what we do,' he added, trying to make it up to his little sister.

'I want an apple,' said Alice.

'Ooh yes, what a wizard wheeze!' shouted Algie. 'Scrumping!'

'Are you sure we should?' cautioned Col. 'Those apples belong to Farmer Tregowan. Wouldn't it be stealing?'

'Not really,' said Algie. 'Look how big the orchard is. We'll only take a few, he'll never miss them.'

'And I do so love apples,' said Alice.

'Then that's settled,' decided Ginger. 'Scrumping it is!' and everyone shouted Hoorah! 'We'll pack up the picnic first so as not to leave the countryside in a mess, and then sneak into the orchard through that hole in the fence over there. I say, I don't know about the rest of you chaps, but I'm trembling all over with excitement.'

'Me too,' said Algie. 'How about you Stinker?'

'Woof!' said Stinker. Well, if Stinker approved it had to be a perfectly capital notion!

The Chipper Chums crept into the orchard through

the hole in the fence and ran over to the apple trees. Stinker leapt up at the shiny, red apples and started to bark.

'Sssh,' said Col, taking hold of Stinker's collar. 'You'll give the game away, old boy. You must keep quiet or Farmer Tregowan will find us.' Stinker hung his tail between his legs. 'If you sit still, I'll bring you an apple,' but the trees were very high and the apples were just out of Col's reach.

'How are we going to pick them?' he asked.

'I could climb up and knock them down to you,' offered Sam.

'Do you think you could?' said Ginger, in amazement. 'I mean you are only a girl.'

'Do you want me to slap you?' said Sam, 'like the time I beat up Dick Stick?' Ginger realised his mistake.

'I'm most dreadfully sorry,' he said, for the third time that day. 'I think it's a famous idea, Sam. Let's give it a whirl.' So Sam started to climb the nearest tree. Even though she was big and strong, however, she only got halfway up before she slid back down the trunk and landed with a bump on the ground.

'Don't worry, old girl,' said Col. 'It was jolly brave of you to try.'

'I think I have it!' shouted Algie. 'Do you remember that circus that came to town two weeks ago?' They all nodded their heads and gathered closer to hear Algie's corking plan. 'And do you remember those fearless acrobats who performed those death-defying stunts? As I recall, in one of their tricks a pretty girl balanced on a man's shoulders.' The gang gasped.

'I remember that now,' said Col. 'It looked really dangerous. Do you think we could do it?'

'I don't see why not,' said Ginger, confidently. 'Who's the tallest here?' It was Sam. 'All right, so who wants to stand on Sam's shoulders?' The boys looked at each other, nervously.

'I'll do it!' said Algie, bravely. 'After all, it was my idea.'

'Well done,' said Ginger. 'Good luck!' and everyone shook Algie's hand, while Sam bent down by the apple tree and waited for Algie to scamper up her back.

Algie's plan worked! Standing on Sam's shoulders he was ten feet tall and the apples were easily within his grasp. He dropped them into the outstretched arms of his pals below and they crunched through the crisp outer skin with gusto. The apples were delicious. Firm and red and juicy.

But, just as Algie had jumped down off Sam's shoulders and was chomping through his own apple, a gunshot cracked through the orchard and a deep, gruff voice shouted, 'You there! What does tha think tha's doing?' The Chipper Chums froze with fear. It was Farmer Tregowan, appearing out of nowhere with a shotgun over his arm. 'Stealing my apples, is ya?' Nobody dared to answer. If Alice's legs had not been so tiny, they would have made a run for the hole in the fence, but they couldn't leave Alice alone to fight off the farmer. Stinker rose to his feet as Farmer Tregowan bore down on the chums. The hackles on the back of his neck stood up and he bared his teeth.

'Sit, Stinker,' commanded Col, but Stinker was protecting his friends from this menacing stranger. He growled at Farmer Tregowan warning him to keep his distance.

'Tell that dog o' yours to stay away fro' me,' said the man with the gun, but Stinker was having none of his threats. He leapt at the farmer, snarling and snapping, trying to drive him off, to give the gang time to make their escape.

'Stinker!' shouted Col, but it was too late. Farmer Tregowan had cocked his gun and fired two cartridges at point blank range into Stinker's chest. The dog slumped to the ground and never moved again.

'Gosh,' said Col. 'I say, that was a pretty rotten thing to do. Poor Stinker! You've no right to go around killing dogs, you know. I shall tell my father.'

'You's can tell who ee likes, but tha's been stealing what's mine. Them's my apples you's been eating.'

'Now look here,' said Algie. 'We're frightfully sorry and all that for scrumping, but there's no need to take that tone with us. We're children. So be a good chap and put that gun down, before it goes off, accidentally.'

The farmer grinned through his stubbly beard. How uncouth he looked, Sam thought, dirty and rough, the sort of man the police were always chasing. But she kept her thoughts to herself.

'Please let us go,' she said. 'Alice here is only three years old.'

'But if I lets ee go, how does I get my apples back? I needs every apple I's got for my cider.'

'How about you give us a cracking good clip round the ear and then we forget all about it?' asked Ginger.

'A biffing box on the nose and let us go,' added Col. 'Fair's fair.'

'No,' said the farmer, grabbing Alice by the scruff of her neck. 'I wants my apples back.'

'But we've eaten them,' said Alice, as she dangled off the farmer's thick wrist.

'Then I shall just have to squeeze 'em out, won't I?'

Col thought that the time had come to stop this silly game once and for all. 'Mr Tregowan,' he said. 'In case you hadn't noticed, we'll all strapping young boys and girls. You can't possibly keep us here. We can run away whenever we like.'

'There won't be no runnings away,' smiled the farmer. 'I's coated my apples with insecticide. One bite and the biter's paralysed in five minutes and don't go running nowhere *never again*!'

The children grasped their throats as the poison took effect. What a perfectly horrible man this farmer was, really mean and unforgiving. Despite all their intentions to escape, he had them just where he wanted – lying helplessly on the ground, unable to move their limbs or open their mouths to shout for help.

Farmer Tregowan bundled the Chipper Chums into the trailer on the back of his tractor and drove them back to his cowshed, where he reclaimed his stolen apples by crushing the children, one by one, in his cider press. He extracted the apple juice from their stomachs and threw their dried out remains into a large, old, oak vat, where the children slowly fermented into that year's brew.

So, if you see a bottle of Tregowan's Vintage Cider from 1952, don't drink it, unless, of course, you're partial to a little extra body in your tipple.

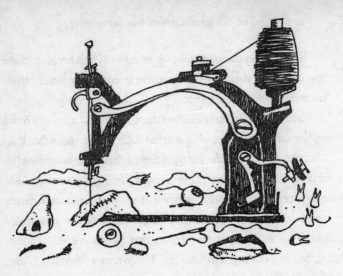

Prince Noman

There were no flowers in this desert where tumbleweed rolled lazily across the parched plains like ghostly tractor wheels, lizards sun-baked in the searing heat and three drops of water made a man rich. In the middle of this scorching inferno stood a walled town called Misery, and inside its four crumbling sandstone towers, a palace, in which there lived a king and a queen who went by the name of Volgar. He was old and crumpled like a damp ermine cloak that had lain too long in a trunk in the attic, but she was young and beautiful and was possessed of sturdy child-bearing hips, which was just as well, because the antique king needed a son and heir, sharpish.

The Volgar family had been big in Misery for five centuries. For the last three hundred years they had ruled unchallenged, enforcing their will on the people through fear and brutality, but the king was close to death and the family knew that without an heir to the throne, the Volgar name would disappear from the history books forever, like a short-legged camel in a sandstorm. And so, on the king's ninety-sixth birthday, a bride had been chosen for him by his moustachioed sister, the indomitable Princess Florrie. A young peasant seamstress called Letitia had been plucked from her parents' home by the Volgar's black-shirted guards, and carried screaming and kicking to the palace dungeons. The wedding had taken place that very same day in the palace chapel and the family had gathered round to bill and coo at the loving couple – the ancient king, drooling in his bath chair and his fresh-faced bride, manacled to the altar rail by her wrists and ankles.

One year later, on a bright summer morning, as the sky skimmed with vultures and the desert floor cracked like a jigsaw, Queen Letitia gave birth to a baby boy. The Volgars celebrated their family's salvation for seven days and seven nights, until the royal wine cellars ran dry and the banqueting halls groaned to the sound of bursting stomachs and trumpeting snores. Never in the history of the whole universe had the birth of a small prince been so keenly awaited by a family of debauched despots.

The baby was snatched away from the queen and handed round the court like a parcel. Argumentative aunts, unctuous uncles and chattering cousins loomed up close to the baby, shoving their blackened teeth, their pinched lips, their hooked noses and their thick, hairy moles into his frightened face.

'Isn't he sweet!' squeaked Princess Florrie. 'He's got my mouth.'

'Yes, but he's got my dreamy, green eyes!' spluttered wine-sodden Uncle Igor.

'And his sticky-out ears are like mine!' twittered Grandma Wilhemina, pinching them between her cold, blue fingers. Her fat sister, Aunt Wildebeest, slapped her hand away.

'No they're not!' she squawked. 'They're like mine!'

'Go boil your head!' snapped Grandma Wilhemina. 'I saw them first!'

'Oh look, he's got my crooked teeth!' roared Cousin Theo.

'You stupid man!' spat Princess Florrie. 'Babies don't have teeth.'

'He's got my pink gums then,' sulked Cousin Theo.

'And my wellborn chin,' gushed the Marquess of Boot. 'All in all he's every bit a Volgar.'

'Er . . . excuse me,' apologised a tiny voice from the far end of the throne room, 'but doesn't he look like me?' It was Queen Letitia. 'He is my baby after all.'

'*Was*,' sneered Princess Florrie. '*Was*, my little peasant girl. He's a Volgar now!'

And all the while, the king was going ga-ga in his bath chair.

'What shall we call our son?' enquired the queen of her frail husband the next day, as she tucked the tartan rug neatly under his knobbly knees. 'Del?'

'He's a prince,' croaked the crumbling king, dribbling into his tin bib. 'He needs a name that will inspire men to heroic deeds. A strong name, a bold name, a name like . . .' He thought for a moment, sending his rheumy eyes into a dreamy spin, '. . . a name like, mine!'

'Norman?' queried the queen, who liked her husband's name even less than she liked her husband.

'Norman!' coughed the king. 'Nothing nobler.'

The queen protested. 'But what about Ronnie or Stan or Elvis? Now Elvis, there's a name!'

'Norman!' reiterated the king, who would not have his decision challenged. 'My son shall be called Norman and there's an end to it.'

Had that been an end to it, this story might never have been told, but three days later, at the official naming ceremony attended by dignitaries from all four corners of the earth, the king, in his dotage, made a tiny slip that was to cast a dark shadow over the prince's life and plunge the Volgar dynasty into terminal decline.

The king forgot his reading glasses. Come the auspicious moment when he was called upon to announce the baby's name, he discovered that he had left his spectacles in the soap rack across the bath and was therefore unable to focus on the crib sheet for his speech. Two strapping young courtiers supported him on either arm as he tottered up the aisle to the cathedral pulpit and cleared his throat. The crowds outside awaited the naming of their new prince with bated breath.

'I name my son,' declared the king, peering closely at the blurred text in front of him, 'I name my son . . . Noman.' The gasp from the Volgar family mushroomed up to the vaulted ceiling like a nuclear blast. Loyal subjects fainted in the streets.

'Noman?' exclaimed Queen Letitia.

'NOMAN?' bristled Princess Florrie's furry top lip.

'That's what it says here,' explained the weak-eyed monarch. 'So Noman he shall be!'

Oh calamity! For, as you all know, a man called Noman very swiftly becomes no man at all. Within a week, to the Volgar's dismay, Noman developed those tell-tale signs of invisibility. No waist with which to hold his trousers up; feetless socks that dangled off his legs like sausage skins with the meat sucked out; and a pale skin that grew paler by the day, until one night, when the Royal Nanny lay him naked on the sofa to change his nappy she saw straight through him and Noman became a cushion cover.

The Royal Doctor was called to examine Noman, but his medical equipment proved useless. Unable to ascertain which way up the invisible prince was, he couldn't even take his temperature, in case he stuck his thermometer in the wrong end. The Royal Cook was ordered to prepare vats of semolina (Noman's favourite food) in the hope that it might put some flesh on him, but the semolina just plopped straight through the prince and made a mess on the floor. Uncle Igor even asked the Royal Bodybuilder to come and build the prince a new body, but when the Royal Bodybuilder pointed out that this was not what a bodybuilder did, Princess Florrie had his head chopped off.

The Volgars were fuming, for a see-through prince was no prince at all, and no prince meant no prizes. Their five hundred year old reign of terror looked set for an early bath. It seemed that nobody could prevent Prince Noman from reaching his vanishing point.

That didn't stop Queen Letitia from trying though. She stole thirty lead slates from the chapel roof and cut an old pink bath towel into the shape of a Babygro. Then she stitched the lead into the suit and popped Noman inside, sprinkling him with water from a garden hose, before pinning him out on the washing line to dry. The lead-lined Babygro shrank to a perfect fit and clung to Noman's fleshless body like a magic outer skin, rendering every part of him visible again . . . every part of him, that is, except his face, for the queen had adapted a small balaclava to cover Noman's head and as we all know balaclavas have a hole at the front where the wind gets in.

Nonetheless, face or no face, Noman's re-bulked body was rapturously received by the Court and proved most timely, because the old king took a sudden turn for the worse during his mid-morning coma and woke up believing he was Florence Nightingale, and as anyone will tell you, a king who is two gems short of a crown is about as much use to his country as a plague of frogs. The Royal Doctor pronounced him a fruitcake and told the Volgars to find a new monarch.

Queen Letitia was summoned to the Great Oval Office of Power.

'Prince Noman will become king tomorrow morning,' barked the whiskery Princess Florrie. The Volgar family wobbled their fat necks in agreement.

'But he still has no face,' protested Queen Letitia. 'What will the people of Misery think when their new king appears on the balcony with nothing between his ears?'

'You're right,' conceded Princess Florrie, 'faceless kings are not popular. You'll just have to make him one.'

'Me?' blurted the queen. 'Make a face? Out of what? I'm not a surgeon. I'm a seamstress.'

'You have until tomorrow morning,' said Princess Florrie, scratching the five o'clock shadow underneath her nose, 'or I'll have you buried alive in a scorpion's nest.'

And that, as the people of Misery had learnt to their cost, was a promise.

That night the palace was as silent as a tomb. A shadowy figure tiptoed through the west wing, flitting in and out of the Volgar's bedrooms like a ghost. Outside, the moon slipped behind a cloud. The desert was black and still, exhausted by the fierce heat of the day.

A light blazed out from a tiny window at the top of the palace's golden tower, like a lighthouse in a storm. It came from the queen's private sewing-room. The door opened and Queen Letitia crept in, carrying her bright red pinking-shears in one hand and a bulging, brown sack in the other. She sat down next to her sewing basket and, by the upright flame of a small white candle, threaded a length of pink cotton through the eye of a darning needle. Then, whilst all around her slept the sleep of the dead, she rebuilt Prince Noman's face, gristly piece by gristly piece.

The palace bustled back to life at dawn, as it had done every morning for three hundred years. Only this particular morning was different. The Volgars refused to come out of their bedrooms until all of the mirrors had been removed from the palace.

Up in her sewing-room, Queen Letitia had finished her work and she laid her needle down next to her pinking-shears. On her lap Prince Noman lay asleep, his tiny mouth fluttering open and closed as he dreamed.

By lunchtime a huge crowd had gathered outside the palace, anxious for news of the king. When Queen Letitia appeared on the balcony cradling a small pink bundle in her arms the crowd fell silent.

'The king is dead,' she announced. 'Long live Prince Noman!'

'But Prince Noman is invisible!' shouted a spectator, boldly. 'He can't be king if nobody can see him.'

'Says who?' cried Queen Letitia. 'Look for yourselves!' As she raised her son above her head, the gasps were heard as far away as Katmandu.

'He has a face!' trilled Molly the mirage-maker. 'Isn't he handsome?'

'Such a family resemblance,' said the snake-butcher's wife. 'He's got Princess Florrie's mouth, God love him!'

'And Uncle Igor's dreamy, green eyes!' added Pugh, the rain-collector.

'His sticky-out ears are just like Grandma Wilhemina's,' called the voice of Misery Radio from the back.

'No they're not,' argued Tom the camel-wash attendant. 'They look like Aunt Wildebeest's.'

'For sure, he's got Cousin Theo's pink gums,' bellowed Ms Pellet the goat-squeezer.

'And the Marquess of Boot's wellborn chin,' added a small scruffy boy at the front, tumbling off his bike as the crowd surged forward to hail their new prince. The queen kissed her baby son on his moustachioed top lip.

'You know,' she smiled, 'they're right, little Noman. All in all, you really are *every bit* a Volgar!'

From that day to this, Queen Letitia has ruled over Misery with compassion and understanding, preparing her beloved son for the day when he is old enough to succeed her as King Noman the First. And the Volgars, what of them? Since that moonless night they have refused to show their faces in public. They have become no-men, living alone in their shuttered bedrooms, shunning the light and the company of other human beings.

If you're still wondering why, I'll tell you a joke that everyone in Misery finds very funny.

> My dog Volgar's got no nose.
> How does he smell?
> He can't. I just told you, he's got no nose.

Death by Chocolate

Why Flies' eyes
Are twice the size
Of Desperate Dan's
Immense cow pies,
Is for a reason plain and clear;
To keep a watch to front and rear.
Whilst supping up at supper time,
(Like sewage workers sucking slime),
Flies' eyeballs keep them on their toes
To help avoid the swatters' blows.

Great brown rivers of the stuff gushed out of the stainless

steel funnel and flooded the cold metal tray with a thick creamy coating of sweet temptation. The man in the white overalls lifted the tray off the bench and replaced it with an empty one, before carrying the full tray over to Mildred Sax, chief cutter-upper at the Squarebush Sou'wester Chocolate factory.

'So how's it looking?' asked Mr Squarebush of his partner.

'Good, Harry. Very good,' smiled Mr Sou'wester. 'Sales of chocolate bunnies are up twenty per cent on this time last year.'

'In that case, I'd like to propose a toast,' announced Mr Squarebush, rising from his seat at the top of the boardroom table. 'Gentlemen, I give you Squarebush Sou'wester bunnies. May they continue to multiply like their real cousins!' The board of directors laughed at their chairman's annual quip and raised their glasses to the best Easter sales yet for Squarebush Sou'wester Chocolate.

Back on the factory floor, Pip Pipkin was greasing the bunny moulds for the next steaming batch of liquid chocolate, when he heard a buzzing in his left ear.

'Buzz off!' he exclaimed, striking out with his arms in a useless attempt to bring down his airborne persecutor, but all he succeeded in doing was knocking the lever that opened the valve on the pipe that carried the chocolate from the blending vat to the moulds on the conveyor belt. Only trouble was, because Pip Pipkin was still greasing them, the moulds weren't on the conveyor belt, so there was nothing to catch the flood of chocolate as it gushed out of the vat.

'What's going on?' roared the foreman, Mr Macgregor. 'Turn that valve off!' Chocolate was squirting out of the nozzle like oil from a gusher, spraying the factory floor and the skidding workforce in sticky, brown gunge. Pip Pipkin was trying to stem the tide by sticking his finger in the end of the pipe, but his efforts created a twenty foot high chocolate fountain that only made matters worse.

'I'm sorry, Mr Macgregor,' he whimpered, as his boss stormed over. 'I don't know what happened. There was a fly buzzing round my ears and I must have knocked the tap by accident!'

'A what?' boomed Mr Macgregor. The factory floor fell silent, save for one tidal roar of spurting chocolate.

'A fly,' whispered Pip Pipkin, shamefully. Mr Macgregor's face switched instantly from purple rage to ashen horror.

'Sound the alarm!' he bellowed, closing the tap on the chocolate pipe.

'Shut down all machinery! There's a fly in the factory!' A loud, piercing siren screamed through the building, as the workers ran backwards and forwards like headless chickens, shouting.

'We'll all lose our jobs, we'll all lose our jobs! Who let the fly in?'

Mr Squarebush heard the alarm and dropped his glass of champagne. 'That's a fly,' he said, flatly. 'Gentlemen, we have a crisis on our hands!'

The executives knocked knees together underneath the boardroom table, while Mr Sou'wester pressed the button on the intercom and said, sternly, 'Miss Filer, call out the SWAT squad.' Then he turned back to the sea of frightened faces and issued a warning. 'If we don't catch this chocolate-fly soon, it could be curtains for Squarebush and Sou'wester.' The suits with the knitted brows gasped in horror. 'If this insect lays its eggs in the main chocolate tank . . . well I don't have to tell you, gentlemen. We'll have to destroy every bunny in the building!'

For Squarebush and Sou'wester, a chocolate-fly laying its eggs in their chocolate was equivalent to a dairy farmer discovering Mad Cow Disease in his herd, or a cabinetmaker detecting Death Watch Beetle in his wood, or an ordinary man in the street finding a tapeworm in his gut. Market research proved that delicious chocolate containing dead flies was not what the public wanted.

The SWAT squad scoured the factory floor with their fly swats at the ready, but they came out empty-handed.

'The chocolate-fly has gone, sir,' said Sergeant Sweety, confidently, to Mr Squarebush.

'But how can you know for sure?' worried Mr Sou'wester.

'Because we're a crack squad of professional men highly

69

trained in the skills of swatting and splatting, sir,' replied
the stiff-jawed sergeant. 'It's our business to know.' And
with that he withdrew his men from the factory floor and
the production line of chocolate bunnies ground back into
gear.

'I hope he's right,' muttered Mr Sou'wester. 'I wouldn't
like to find a maggot in my Easter chocolate.'

'No,' nodded Mr Squarebush. 'No, neither would I.'

From high up on the gantry, directly above Pip Pipkin's
position, the cunning chocolate-fly dropped an egg into
an unfilled bunny mould before flying out of the open
window as buzzlessly as it could.

The bunny containing the egg was given to a girl called
Serena Slurp. Serena was a great big tub of a girl, with
mean little eyes and a splodge of a nose right in the middle
of her chubby cheeks. She hadn't always been vast, but
over the last few years she had developed a secret passion
for chocolate and had taken to stashing bars all over the
house so that she was never far away from a fix. Serena was
a chocoholic. She needed chocolate like you or I need
water to quench our thirsts. She'd eat chocolate cakes and
biscuits, chocolate spread sandwiches, chocolate peanuts
and raisins, chocolate ice-cream and even the poor dog's
choc drops when times were lean. Once, she woofled down
a plateful of chocolate ants, in spite of the fact that they
wouldn't stay still when she scooped them on to her fork

and ran up her nose and hid in her ears.

She loved her chocolate any which way; dark, white or milky, in a bar, on a stick or licked off the back of a stranger's hand (she'd done that once to a man sitting next to her on a bus and had received some very peculiar looks). Chocolate milkshakes, chocolate hundreds and thousands and hot chocolate drinks, cooking chocolate, chocolate creams, chocolate sauce and once, by accident, a chocolate laxative bar, which kept her running to the loo for a fortnight. Feeding Serena was not a problem as long as she could have chocolate on her food. Imagine eating chocolate fish and chips or roast chocolate chicken or even chocolate hot pot – disgusting! But not for Serena. Chocolate was her cream dream and she couldn't get enough of it.

She had a younger sister called Eli, a pretty, little slip of a thing who never said boo to a goose. But Eli lived in the shadow of her brutal big sister who persecuted her from morning till night, demanding favours in exchange for not telling Mummy about Eli's misdemeanours. Things like spilling a teaspoon of milk on the breakfast table.

'Whoops!' said Eli.

'Oh dear,' gasped Serena, cruelly. 'What *have* you done, Eli?'

'I'll clear it up.'

'Too late for that now. If you don't go into the larder and steal me a chocolate biscuit, I'll tell Mummy how you threw that milk on the table deliberately.'

'But I didn't,' blubbed Eli.

'Shall we let Mummy decide?' threatened Serena.

'Oh all right then, I'll get your stupid chocolate!'

But if Eli was caught, Serena would pretend she knew nothing about it. She'd shake her head disapprovingly and say in her grown-up voice, 'Honestly, you should be ashamed of yourself Eli, stealing biscuits from the larder when you know Mummy doesn't approve!'

Four months had passed since Easter. It was August and the country was wilting from the hottest summer since records began. The town where Serena and Eli lived was plagued by swarms of black flies which thrived in the heat, feasting like ragamuffin kings from dustbins full of bad meat and rotting vegetables, and sucking the sweat from the skin of sticky human beings.

Serena and Eli's mother bought a fly swat to do battle with the flies. Eli thought it was grand and commandeered it for herself, wearing it through her trouser belt like a Samurai sword, and using it to stalk her winged foe through the house. She had very little success, though. The flies were always too quick for her, but Eli loved the swish and the thwack of the swat and spent most of her school holidays happily hunting. Serena on the other hand, devoted *her* time to freezing bars of chocolate in the fridge. The sun was not kind to her favourite food, liquifying it into large, brown puddles if she happened to leave it on a window-ledge by mistake.

Into the fridge she also put her chocolate Easter bunny. Eli had eaten hers the moment she'd been given it, but Serena was one of those annoying children who save their Easter eggs to eat later. She'd wait six months, until Eli was nice and jealous of the egg and then eat it in front of her, slowly and deliberately, savouring every mouthful, teasing her drooling younger sister with each tantalising no-you-can't-have-any lick.

The summer drifted by happily enough with both girls staying out of each other's way, until the day that Eli snapped the fly swat. She was chasing a juicy bluebottle through the sitting-room when she saw a rather old and weary looking fly limping along the back of the sofa. Here was her chance. She couldn't squash the fit ones, but a three-legged fly was a sitting duck. She raised the swat high above her head, narrowed her eyes and delivered a vicious blow to the fly's head that would have been fatal had not the fly lazily buzzed off just before she struck. The result of her brute force, however, was to snap the fly swat in half. Eli gulped. She hadn't meant to do it. It was an accident. She decided it would be better to keep the breakage a secret and was just laying the fly swat out on the coffee-table (pushing the two ends together to make it look unbroken) when Serena walked in and caught her.

'Oh dear,' came the familiar, scheming tones of Eli's big sister. 'What have we got here?'

'I didn't do it,' shouted Eli.

'Yes you did, little sister,' smiled Serena, wagging her finger at Eli.

'Who's a naughty girl, then?' Eli bit her lip. She knew what was coming next. 'What do you think Mummy will say when she sees this?' said Serena, holding up the broken fly swat in both hands. 'She'll be so angry!'

'Please don't tell her,' begged Eli.

'I might and I might not,' said Serena, casually. 'It depends.'

'On what?' trembled Eli.

'On whether you'll be my slave or not!'

'No,' protested Eli. 'I'm your sister.'

'OK then. MUMMY!' Serena shouted as loud as she could and would have done so again, had Eli not slapped her hand over Serena's mouth.

'All right, all right, all right, all right!' she squealed, with tears in her eyes. 'I'll be your slave.'

'What is it?' asked their mother, entering the sitting-room through the French windows. 'What do you want?'

'Nothing,' smiled Serena sweetly, hiding the fly swat behind her back. 'I thought I saw a hornet, that's all.' Her mother grunted and eyed her two daughters suspiciously before returning to her gardening. Eli wanted to go with her, but Serena grabbed her arm. She had a wicked glint in her eye.

'Right,' she said smugly, licking her puffy lips with

sadistic relish. 'What shall I get my slave to do first?'

The next week was pure misery for Eli. She waited on Serena hand and foot; sitting on the loo seat to warm it up before Serena used it, folding her sister's clothes, tidying her room, running her bath, fixing the brakes on her bike, brushing her hair, spoon-feeding her Coco Pops at breakfast and, of course, fetching her chocolate from the fridge. One day, after Eli had just delivered a wheelbarrowful of Smarties to Serena's bedside, their mother caught Serena being sick in the bathroom.

'I feel awful,' moaned the greedy guzzler with a chocolate moustache.

'Well, you've only got yourself to blame,' said her mother, sharply. 'Your eyes are bigger than your stomach!' But Serena didn't listen. She became so lazy that she lay on the sofa all day like a Roman emperor and when Eli stamped her foot and said she'd had enough of being a slave, Serena simply produced the broken fly swat from behind a cushion and raised her eyebrows quizzically, as if to say, 'Well? Shall I?' And Eli's answer was always no.

Then, two days before they went back to school, a strange thing happened. The weather got even hotter and all of the chocolate bars in all of the shops in all of the towns in all of the counties, melted. There wasn't a single chocolate bar left in the whole country. Eli knew, because Serena had sent her out on a frantic search to find one, with strict instructions not to return until she had. Eli had tried fifty-four shops before she had given up. She came home in tears, because she had failed her big sister.

'I'm sorry,' she wailed. 'I did try my best. I did! Don't tell Mummy.' Serena's face was black with rage. She hadn't tasted chocolate now for at least an hour.

'Bring me my bunny!' she growled. She'd been saving the Easter bunny for a really special occasion, but needs must when the devil drives. Her chocolate craving was like a roaring giant in her belly demanding to be fed. 'Faster!' she bawled, as Eli ran to the fridge and whipped out her sister's fix. Serena was no longer interested in teasing Eli with the chocolate bunny, speed was of the essence now; to cram it down her gob as fast as she possibly could. She ripped off the cellophane wrapping with her teeth and stuffed the chocolate ears deep into her throat, tearing them off the bunny's head like a wild dog.

Suddenly, Eli noticed a small white maggot wriggling out of the bunny's chewed neck.

'Ugh!' she screamed. 'Serena, stop! Look! Ugh! It's a wiggly thing!'

'Shut up,' glowered Serena. 'Can't you see I'm eating?'

'But there's a maggot in the bunny.'

'You're just saying that so I'll give you some!' leered Serena. 'Well I won't. It's mine!'

'But there's a mag—' Eli gagged. Serena had just chomped through the bunny's shoulders and gulped down the maggot, whole. Eli left the room to be sick.

And that was how the maggot came to be inside Serena. When it arrived in her stomach, it discovered a lake of bubbling chocolate so deep that it was able to feast for a fortnight, transforming its short, squeeze-box body into that of a giant chocolate-fly, which devoured its host's body from within and sucked out her brain.

When Eli went into Serena's bedroom, two weeks later, she discovered a chocolate-fly sitting up in bed staring at her. She screamed and ran away, but the fly flew out from under Serena's duvet and chased her downstairs.

'Get away!' cried Eli, picking up the broken fly swat. 'Leave me alone! I shall squish you!' Then to Eli's surprise, the fly spoke.

'It's me, Serena,' it said. 'Don't be frightened.'

'It's a trick,' screamed Eli. 'You're a fly!'

'I'm your sister.'

'No you're not, you're a monster!'

'Don't you recognise your own flesh and blood?' pleaded the fly. 'Eli, I AM Serena. Look, my eyes are bigger than my stomach.'

'That's because you're a fly,' wailed Eli. 'All flies have eyes like saucepan lids.' Then she panicked and lashed out with the swat and squashed her vicious sister into a huge black mess on the carpet.

'What's going on?' said Eli's mother, appearing suddenly in the doorway. Eli froze over the splodged corpse of the chocolate-fly. 'Eli?' Eli blinked.

'I think I've just broken the fly swat,' she said, holding up both ends in her bloody hands.

'Oh,' said her mother. 'Is that all? I thought it was something serious.'

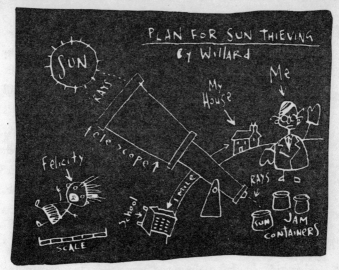

Well'ard Willard

Once upon a time there was a boy who couldn't tell the truth. No, I tell a lie. He could tell the truth, but sometimes he chose not to. The boy's name was Willard. Willard wore glasses and combed his hair flat across his forehead like Adolf Hitler. Willard was a boffin. A science freak, who had turned his bedroom into a laboratory, where he conducted ear-shattering experiments in the middle of the night, filling the still air with bubblings and clankings and fizzings and phlumps. He also had a telescope. Not a yo-ho-ho-and-a-bottle-of-rum type of telescope like Nelson put to his good eye, but a huge, whacking great gun barrel of a thing. A vast, tubular cannon that sat in the middle of the garden, like a lighthouse on a tripod, and pointed up into space. Willard loved his telescope. He loved to sit out in the garden on clear balmy nights and gaze at the stars till the early morning sun bleached them out of the sky. His parents encouraged this hobby and were proud of their darling boy. As far as they were concerned, he never lied, he never kept secrets and he loved his mother and father. He was as close to perfect as it's possible for a boy to be. But this was at home, you understand. At school, he was quite different.

At Willard's school, scientists were labelled as weirdos. Other kids avoided them in the corridor for fear of catching the *science bug*. You know the symptoms; pallid, grey skin from spending all day in darkened laboratories, thin, podgy limbs from never playing sport, and a complete disregard for personal appearance, their heads too full of calculi and theorem to worry about their unzipped flies, their untucked shirts and their different-coloured socks. At Willard's school scientists were wimpy ginks. So, at school, Willard changed who he was, to make sure other kids liked him. He became Well'ard Willard, the toughest nut in the class, the fearless boy who had done everything, been everywhere and met Cindy Crawford on a plane.

'Oh yeah, she offered me a peanut. Straight up. I'm not lying.' The others were so impressed by Willard's tall stories that he was elevated to chief cheese in the school, which basically meant that he was very popular and could sit where he liked at lunch. This is the story of Well'ard Willard's last lie. The one that wouldn't stop growing. The one that turned round and whacked him dead.

'I've driven motorbikes, me. Oh yeah. I can ride them with my eyes closed. Barry Sheen offered me a million quid to turn professional, but I told him it wasn't enough.' Well'ard Willard was addressing a group of thirty sad saps in the playground. 'I can eat fifteen boiled eggs in three minutes, you know. Not even Margaret Thatcher can do that. I've met her. During the Falklands war. I commanded a tank regiment. She awarded me a medal, but I gave it away to Battersea Dogs' Home. Do you know what they do there? They barbecue the stray dogs for dinner. I've set hundreds of them free. Oh yeah, I'm a great wildlife supporter me. Saved a tiger from a bush fire in the Hindu Kush once.' The spellbound faces in Willard's audience lapped up his fibs like thick chocolate sauce. 'Have you heard? When I'm fifteen, I'm going into space. First boy astronaut in the world, that's me. And I can eat three Shredded Wheat.'

'Really?' gawped his gullible fans.

'I learned how to do it in prison.'

'You've been in prison?' exclaimed Sebastian.

'Armed robbery,' lied Well'ard Willard. 'But I'm not proud of what I did. I was naive and impressionable in those days.' *A bit like you dozy lot*, he thought to himself.

'Have none of you ever stolen anything?' The crowd of boys giggled.

'I once took a tissue from Mummy's handbag,' admitted Arnold, shamefully.

'Child's play,' mocked Well'ard Willard.

'I stole a kiss from Amanda,' giggled Jonathan, but Willard cut him dead with a glare. When he was being hard, Willard never smiled.

'I've stolen a Mars bar,' said Simeon. Willard snorted, like they were all babies and out of his league.

'That's nothing,' he said. 'I've stolen the sun.' A reverential hush fell over his audience. Jaws clanged open, eyes corkscrewed on to cheeks, tongues flopped out like dead fish.

'Wow!' gasped the all-believing crowd. 'That's mega!' Actually, Willard had quite impressed himself. It was the biggest and best lie he'd ever told. He'd have to remember to tell it again.

'So what's that big, yellow shiny thing in the sky then?' said a voice, unexpectedly. It belonged to a new girl called Felicity who was listening to Willard's stories for the first time. The hard man squirmed. He'd never been rumbled before, but he couldn't admit to his friends that he was lying or they wouldn't be his friends any more. He was in a spot and he stalled for time.

'Are you calling me a liar?' he said, unimpressively.

'Yes. If you've stolen the sun, why's it still up there?'

'That's a model,' fabricated Willard, 'that I made . . . erm . . . out of string and wood and an extra strong lightbulb. I've got the real one at home.'

'Tosh!' said Felicity. 'You're lying. Your ears have gone red.'

'That's because you're giving me earache!' side-stepped Willard, but he knew he'd just reached a turning point. If Felicity didn't ask to see the stolen sun his lie would go undetected, but if she wanted proof he'd be in a whole jar of a pickle.

'All right, let's see this sun, then,' she said. Willard wanted to punch Felicity right on the end of her nose.

'Can't!' he bluffed. 'Mum and Dad have got leprosy so nobody's allowed in our house for the next ten years.'

'Then bring it into school,' said the girl. Willard's tongue twisted into knots. Now that he'd started lying it was impossible to stop, but every time he told another lie, he had to invent an even bigger one to cover his tracks. If she didn't shut up soon, his brain would explode.

'I can't bring the sun into school,' he snapped, crossly, 'because it won't fit in my satchel.'

'Not good enough,' retorted the girl. 'You're just a big liar. You haven't stolen the sun.'

'I have too,' shouted Willard.

'Liar, liar! Pants on fire!' she chanted back, and that was the final nail in his coffin. Willard's adoring fans started to drift off.

'Don't go!' he yelled, but they kept on walking. Alarm bells rang in his head. Dive! Dive! Dive! Common sense told him to tell the truth, but he had his reputation in the playground to protect. He was Well'ard Willard! Head honcho, main man, school supremo. 'All right!' he blustered, halting the crowd's retreat. 'If you want to see my sunbeams, I'll show you!' Now he'd done it.

'Monday morning, then,' said a triumphant Felicity. 'Do bring the sun into school, Willard. I can hardly wait!'

And that was how it started. How Well'ard Willard told one little lie to impress his mates and lived to regret it.

Not for long though.

After school, he rushed home in a panic. His stupid lie meant that he now had two days to steal the sun. It couldn't be done. It wasn't like he could just run up a ladder and pluck it out of the sky. If he'd just kept his big gob shut, none of this mess would ever have happened! And then, while he was moping in the middle of the lawn, leaning on his telescope, he had a brilliant idea.

'Hello Willard, dear,' said his mother, as Willard entered the kitchen.

'Have you got an empty jamjar?' he asked.

'What would that be for, dear?'

'For st—' Willard stopped himself from saying for stealing the sun just in time. His mother was a member of the Neighbourhood Watch and disapproved of theft on principle. There was nothing else for it: 'For some worm-catching,' he said, wincing as he did so, for this was the first time he had ever lied to his mother. 'I might go fishing later.'

'Well you run along and have fun, dear,' she smiled, handing him an empty jamjar, 'but mind you don't catch the sun!' Willard's mouth fell open. How did she know? 'You know how easily your skin burns,' she added.

'Oh, I see!' he said. 'You mean, careful of sunburn.'

'Yes dear. Why? What did you think I meant?'

'Oh, nothing,' replied Willard, casually. The second lie was much easier.

His brilliant idea was this. When he was Well'ard Willard at school, he would often prove his manliness by exploding insects. He'd trap the ants or beetles in a test-tube and magnify the sun's rays through the lenses of his glasses on to their heads – a bit like a home-made laser beam. Well, if he could magnify the sun through his telescope, maybe he could achieve high concentrations of sunbeams in his mum's jamjar.

It was a rubbish theory, but surprisingly it worked. He pointed the telescope at the sun, placed his jamjar over the small, eye-piece end and, seconds later, a hundred sunbeams poured out through the bottom of the telescope and filled up the jar with fine, golden dust, like sieved breadcrumbs.

When the jar was full, Willard slammed on the lid and ran upstairs to study it under his microscope. Each minute speck of dust sparkled like a miniature star and had around its edge a thin circle of yellow light which pulsated like a radioactive halo.

Willard stood up.

'Blimey!' he said, 'I think I've done it. I've burglarised a bit of the sun!' He looked up at the giant, sizzling orb in the sky to see if it looked any smaller. Unfortunately, it didn't, which meant that nicking the whole hot thing was going to require an awful lot of jamjars.

Nonetheless, Willard stuck to his task undaunted, rising at dawn and returning to bed when the last ray of sunshine had dipped down behind the city skyline. He harvested millions of sunbeams in his jamjar and piled the stolen gold dust on a sheet of newspaper underneath his bed. When his parents asked him what he was doing, Willard lied brazenly, for fear that they'd put a stop to it.

'What have you got there, son?' asked his father on Sunday morning.

'A jamjar,' said Willard, slipping the hotpot up his jumper.

'Yes, but what's in it?' persisted his father, peering at Willard over the top of his teacup.

'Air,' replied Willard, slyly.

'And what are you building in your bedroom that's upsetting your mother?'

The question came out of the blue and caught Willard off guard.

'Nothing,' he said.

'It's very hot, dear,' said his mother. 'It's blistering the new paintwork on the landing, and it's very bright as well, like a furnace.'

'Oh that,' fibbed Willard. 'That's a . . . that's a . . .' He wasn't very good at lying to his mother and father. He hadn't had much practice. 'That's a volcano.'

'A volcano!' said his startled father. 'In your bedroom!'

'I mean a sunlamp,' said Willard, hurriedly.

'A sunlamp!' exclaimed his mother. 'How very posh. That would explain why you're burnt down one side of your face.' Willard had noticed the red patches that morning. Sleeping on top of the sun had its drawbacks.

'Be a good lad and close the door for your mother, will you?' said his father. 'The nights are drawing in and she does feel the chill something awful in her varicose veins.'

'I wonder why it's getting dark so early?' said Willard's mother, after Willard had left the room.

'It says in the paper,' explained Willard's father, 'that the sun is shrinking, dear.'

'Is that so, dear?' said Willard's mother.

'Scientists estimate that it will have completely disappeared by this evening!'

'Oh dear, dear,' mumbled Willard's mother. 'Well, I hope they sort it out soon or my tomatoes will be ruined.'

That was nine o'clock on Sunday morning. Six hours later, Willard was still feverishly collecting sunbeams when the world slipped into a state of perpetual darkness. The temperature of the planet plummeted below freezing, while Willard's bedroom soared to a sweltering 2,000 degrees centigrade – hotter than Death Valley, the hottest place on earth, where the sandflies wear insulated boots to stop their feet from burning. At five o'clock, the sun went down for the last time as Willard trapped his final sunbeam. He had achieved the impossible by stealing the sun and could now go into school tomorrow and shame Felicity by proving that he hadn't been lying.

Unfortunately, the next morning he arrived at school with the sun on his back only to find the gates locked. The building had been closed due to frozen pipes. There was nobody there for Well'ard Willard to show off his stolen sun to. His lie, his cover-up, his planetary plundering had all been for nothing. Not only that, but Willard was sunburnt from the top of his head to the tip of his toes. His skin was as red as a fireball, blisters had bubbled up on his face like pneumatic pillows and he was generally more uncomfortable than a barbecued Bambi in a bush blaze.

His parents were sitting by the fire, their pale lips chattering in the icy gloom, when Willard walked in, glowing scarlet like a neon lobster.

'Why are you so sunburnt,' asked his father, 'when everybody else is as grey as a corpse?' Willard couldn't tell his father the truth or he'd be blamed for the death of the planet and he didn't want that guilt hanging round his neck for the rest of his life.

'I've invented a travel machine,' he said, watching his parents closely to see if they'd swallow his porky pie.

'That's nice, dear,' said his mother from behind her newspaper.

'And I've been using it every night for the last week to nip over to Australia to catch some rays . . . I mean, do a bit of sunbathing.'

'That's strange,' puzzled his father. 'I thought Australia had lost its sun too.' Willard tittered nervously.

'Sorry, did I say travel machine? I meant *time* travel machine. I mean, I don't go over to Australia for *today's* sun, obviously, because it's not there. I go back in time, to a time when they had loads of sunshine. That's why I'm sunburnt.'

'Could we see this time travel machine?' asked his mother.

'No,' fidgeted Willard, dodging his mother's awkward question as best he could. 'It only worked once, so I've thrown it away.' She looked up.

'Only worked once? But you just said you'd been to Australia every night for a week.' Willard gulped. Yes, he *had* said that, hadn't he?

'Well, yes, obviously I've been going for a week, but when I said it only worked once, I meant it had only worked *once* there and *once* back. And once I was back, I realised that if it had worked once it would work again, so I used it once more, there and back, and . . . well you know how these things happen . . . I used it once too often and it blew up.'

'And then you threw it away?'

'Is that what I said?' sweated Willard, who couldn't remember which lie he'd told last.

'Yes,' said his father.

'Then that's what I did,' said Willard, gratefully.

'What a shame,' said his father. 'Your mother and I have never seen a time machine before. Was it big, Willard?'

'Huge,' bluffed the boy.

'I suppose that's where the bright light came from, then?'

'What bright light's that?'

'The one I saw shining out of your bedroom window this morning.' And with that, Willard's barrel of lies ran dry. His edifice of deceit collapsed about his ears like a house of cards. He'd forgotten that the sun didn't stop shining just because it was tucked away underneath his bed. Why hadn't he drawn the curtains?

'Oh I say,' shouted his mother, suddenly waving the newspaper in the air. 'Listen to this, dear. They think they know who the thief is.'

'Thief?' said Willard's father.

'The person who stole the sun.' Willard's heart skipped a beat.

'Do they, dear?'

'Yes, and . . . oh dear.' Willard's mother stopped as she read the name of the culprit. Then she looked up with sad, disbelieving eyes. 'They think it's you Willard,' she gasped. 'The police think it's that bright light in your bedroom window.' Now Willard *knew* he should have drawn the curtains!

'Willard,' exclaimed his father. 'Tell me what you know about the theft of the sun.'

'Nothing!' denied Well'ard Willard, who at that precise moment was softer than a box of strawberry creams. Then he squeaked like a frightened mouse and ran upstairs to undo what he should never have done in the first place.

He had to put the sun back. If he could slip it back into the sky without anyone noticing, he could pretend he'd never had it and then they wouldn't send him to prison. To hell with Felicity – she could call him a liar as often as she liked if he could just get rid of this sun! He'd throw it out of his window and trust to luck that sunbeams could travel both ways in space; up as well as down.

He slipped on a pair of his mother's oven gloves, rolled back his mattress and plunged his hands into the dazzling heap of gold dust. Wisps of white smoke trailed off his wrists as he ran to the open window and hurled the first sunbeams into the darkness. They swirled across the garden like a cloud of fireflies, but instead of soaring upwards into the sky they stopped in midair, twenty feet off the ground, and spiralled on the spot, like a spinning hub-cap.

'Willard,' came the voice of Willard's father. His parents were climbing the stairs. 'Your mother and I would like a word.' Now he'd have to hurry.

'Won't be a minute,' he yelled, scooping half of the dust heap into his duvet and staggering to the window.

'Is something burning, dear?' asked his mother.

'No,' lied Willard as his duvet smouldered in his hands. He flapped it out of the window and released a second shower of sunbeams into the night. The sun regained half its normal size, but still refused to rise into the sky. At its centre it was a deathly grey and it dangled coldly over Willard's lawn like the heart of a hanged man.

There was a loud knock at the door. 'Coming!' shouted Willard. He had to get the remaining gold dust out of the window before his parents came in. He tore the carpet from its gripper rods and dragged it across his bedroom floor. Then with one almighty heave, he wrestled the carpet over the windowsill and scattered the last of the sunbeams into the sky. They shimmered across the garden and were sucked into the eye of the sparkling vortex, like a shoal of electric eels slithering down a blue whale's throat.

'Done it!' gasped Willard, turning to the door. 'You can come in now.' But even as he spoke, there was a megaton explosion outside and the sun came back to life, flooding its flashbulb light across the rooftops, shooting sharp shadows over the frozen earth. With a mighty roar, the face of the sun burst into flames, scorching the window where Willard was standing. Before he could move, his blood had reached boiling point. Before he could scream, his body fluids had evaporated. As the sun streaked back into the heavens, Willard drifted slowly after it as tiny droplets of moisture. He disappeared into the earth's atmosphere, leaving only his dry, sunburnt skin as a wrinkled memento for his parents to find when they burst into the room seconds later.

From the outset, Willard had been lying to save his skin. But what use is a skin when there's nothing left to go inside it?

Three months later, Well'ard Willard fell to earth as a warm shower over Madagascar and ended his life as a thirst-quenching drink for a warthog.

Athlete's Foot

The crowd of schoolchildren surged to its feet as the runners swept round the final bend into the home straight. Anthony St John Smythe was in the lead, his long elegant legs pulling him away from the rest of the field, his floppy, blonde hair streaming out behind him, his arrogant smile plastered across his pink face like a wet peach slice in a round bowl of strawberry blancmange. He breasted the tape and raised his hands to acknowledge the cheers. He was All England Schools Champion for the fourth year in a row and he was the best. He knew it, too.

A line of puce-faced panting athletes straggled in behind him. Limp and exhausted they flopped over the finishing line and lay down to catch their breath, whilst out on the track a lone baggy-shorted figure in black elasticated gym shoes padded on. Oliver Littlebody was the runt of the race, a sparrow of a boy with thin, spindly legs and he still had two hundred yards left to run. The crowd laughed as he wound up his rubbery limbs and sprinted for the line like a flat-footed ostrich; arms flapping, knees knocking and cheeks puffing from the effort. With twenty yards to go, he tripped over his own feet and sprawled across the track in front of the grandstand. Anthony St John Smythe broke off from his lap of honour and ran over to Ollie's side, where he pretended to count him out like a boxing referee.

'A one, a two, a three . . .' he mocked, much to the crowd's delight. The inside of Ollie's bottom lip stung, where the cinder track had cut him, but he was no quitter. Fighting back tears of humiliation, he struggled to his feet and staggered over the line. 'You're useless,' Anthony whispered in his ear. 'I don't know why you bother to turn up.'

' 'cause one day I'm going to beat you,' gasped Ollie.

'You couldn't beat a tortoise on crutches,' sneered Anthony. 'Dream on, matchstick boy.' Then he rushed back to his adoring female fans who had leapt over the barriers to get him to autograph their T-shirts.

Ollie cut a despondent figure as he trudged down the tunnel towards the changing-rooms. An old man leant over the wall of the stand and tapped him on the shoulder with his walking-stick.

'Well run,' he said. Ollie stared at him blankly. Either this man was blind or he'd mistaken Ollie for someone else.

'I ran like a three-legged donkey,' he said, but the stranger disagreed.

'You showed real guts out there today. I once knew a boy ran just like you. He was All England Schools Champion back in the 40s.' The old man chuckled. 'Tommy Knock, his name was. Best quarter-miler this country ever produced.'

'Never heard of him,' said Ollie.

'Nobody has,' sighed the old man. 'He was killed during the war, before he had a chance to prove himself.'

Ollie didn't know which war he was talking about and besides his legs ached, so he said, 'Oh,' and left it at that.

'He was a friend of mine,' the old man remembered, sadly. Ollie sucked his sore lip. 'So, let's make a deal.'

'What?' said Ollie, surprised by this sudden change of tack.

'If your parents agree to it, you give me half an hour of your time every day for a year and I'll teach you how to beat Anthony St John Smythe.'

'Me, run faster than God's-Gift-To-Lycra? No way!'

'I said beat him,' repeated the old man. 'This time next year.'

'But he just duffed me up like a snail.'

'You can't win every time,' said the old man, wisely.

'Anthony St John Smythe does,' came Ollie's acid retort.

'Then it's up to you to beat him.' The old man laid down the gauntlet for Ollie to pick up, but the boy hesitated. He wasn't sure. Who was this weird old man? What exactly did he want? Ollie turned for some answers, but the old man had disappeared. All Ollie could hear was the tap tap of the old man's walking-stick and the click of the rusty iron turnstile as he let himself out of the stadium.

The next day after school, when Ollie turned up to meet the old man, the stadium was empty, except for one lonely runner sprinting round and round the track like a hamster on a wheel.

'I knew it,' he mumbled to himself. 'He isn't coming. He doesn't think I can beat Anthony St John Smythe either.' He rested his chin on his hands and studied the athlete on the track. What Ollie wouldn't have given to run like that. Fat chance now! It was time to go home, but just as he turned to leave, the runner called out his name and ran over to greet him.

'You came,' said the old man. Ollie was astonished. The old man was even weedier than he was with a concave body like a dried out rat and scrawny legs that stuck out the bottom of his baggy shorts like Bonsai twigs.

'Was that really you sprinting round the track like an Olympic champion?' he asked. The old man smiled modestly. 'But you're . . . well . . . you're . . .'

'Old,' stated the old man. 'You noticed. There are secrets in this world, Oliver, that even you don't understand.' There was a twinkle in his rheumy eye. 'Now, I believe we had a deal. I'm going to teach you to beat Anthony St John Smythe. Shall we begin?'

The old man bent down and unlaced his black, leather running spikes. 'I want you to start by running round the track as fast as you can,' he said. 'I'll time you.'

'Now?' asked Ollie.

'Now,' said the old man.

Ollie did as he was told, completing the 400 metre circuit in just under two and a half minutes.

'See,' he puffed. 'Pathetic. I'm not built to run fast.' But the old man didn't seem bothered. He ignored Ollie's whingeing and handed him his running shoes.

'Now, try it in these,' he said. The leather was hard and cracked and as black as charcoal. Ollie struggled to squeeze his feet inside.

'I can hardly walk,' he complained, as he hobbled around on the grass. 'It's like wearing clogs.'

'But you don't have to walk, do you?' said the old man. 'Try running in them, Oliver. Once round. I'll time you again.'

'I'll be lucky to get off the starting blocks,' grumbled Ollie, as he tiptoed painfully over to the track and stood on his marks.

'On your marks, get set . . . go!' shouted the old man,

and Ollie set off. It was an extraordinary feeling, like the shoes were alive, like they were hovering over the track on a cushion of air, like there were rockets in his heels. His puny legs were pumping like steam pistons as the shoes flashed him up the back straight and cruised round the top bend. Ollie had never run so fast in his life, his feet had never been this hot, either. It was like running on burning coals. Then suddenly, there it was, the finishing line. The shoes accelerated over the last fifty metres and skipped Ollie home in a new lap record of forty-six seconds flat!

Ollie's feet were gently smoking as the old man limped up to him.

'Now do you believe me?' he grinned. 'In those shoes you can knock Anthony St John Smythe for six!' Ollie was still trying to catch his breath.

'But why?' he asked. 'What's so special about these shoes?'

'They belonged to a friend of mine,' said the old man.

'He's not a dead friend by any chance, is he?' The old man raised an eyebrow. 'Who died in the war?'

'They belonged to Tommy Knock,' confirmed the old man. 'As a matter of fact, he was wearing them when he died.'

'You mean, he died running?'

'During the war,' said the old man, cryptically. 'One day I'll tell you his story, but right now we've got some training to do.'

'Training?' scoffed Ollie. 'There's no need to train if I've got magic shoes.'

'Quite right,' applauded the old man, 'but this is *special* training.'

'Weights, you mean?'

'No. Shopping,' said the old man, producing a scrap of paper from one pocket and a five pound note from the other. 'I want you to go to the supermarket and buy these items.'

'Oh, I see,' said Ollie. 'You're putting me on a special diet.'

'No, you're buying my supper. Baked beans on toast.' Ollie didn't want to appear ungrateful or anything, but he was under the impression that this old man was going to teach him how to run faster than any other human being in the history of the world, not how to go shopping. 'The deal is, you're mine for thirty minutes every evening for the next year.'

'For running,' complained Ollie.

'To show you how to beat Anthony St John Smythe,' corrected the old man. 'And I've already done that.'

'But shopping . . .'

'I'm an old man, Oliver. I walk with a stick. You're young and fit. It seems a perfectly fair swap to me.' Ollie felt like he'd been cheated, but the last thing he wanted was the old man to walk off with the magic shoes. He accepted the new deal on one condition.

'Do you promise the boots will always run as fast as they did just now?'

'You have my word on that,' said the old man. 'Tommy Knock never ran a bad race in his life. The boots simply repeat whatever happened to him. That's their magic.'

'And Tommy Knock *was* the All England Schools Champion, wasn't he?'

'In 1940, yes.'

'What about 1941?' asked Ollie, but the old man avoided this question.

'Now run along and get my beans,' he said. 'I'm famished.'

From then on, their training sessions followed an identical pattern. Ollie would go round to the old man's flat after school to collect a shopping list, some money and occasionally some special-offer coupons. He would then get on the bus and go to the local supermarket where he would buy the old man's dinner – chicken and mushy peas, coley pie and ketchup, sausages and boiled cabbage – whatever took the old boy's fancy. Back in the flat, Ollie would cook the food, wait while the old man ate it, do the washing-up and then go home.

Ollie never complained about his coach's unconventional training methods, but sometimes his face betrayed his disappointment at not being out on the track doing split times and fitness circuits like all the other budding athletes. Whenever this happened the old man would take

Tommy Knock's running spikes out of the shoe box in his fridge and let Ollie try them on, promising him that when the new season started there'd be time enough for Ollie to show the world what he could do in them.

The old man was true to his word. The athletics season began in April the following year and the old man entered Ollie for a succession of races up and down the country. Within a matter of weeks there were two names on everybody's lips: Anthony St John Smythe and Oliver Littlebody. Anthony started the season as favourite to retain his Championship title, but as time wore on, Oliver's consistently brilliant performances brought the two boys level. His old-fashioned smoking spikes were the talking point of locker rooms and newspaper offices throughout the land.

Then one day an article headlined 'By Golly It's Ollie!' appeared in the trade magazine *Track and Field Monthly*. It hailed Oliver Littlebody as the best 400 metres runner this country had ever seen, better by far than his rival Anthony St John Smythe who, by comparison (so the journalist wrote), 'ran like a gangly girl with rickets.' When Anthony read this his vain brain boiled over with jealousy. He and only he was the champion and so he would be again, by fair means or foul! Anthony tore the paper into a thousand tiny pieces and ate it.

'What are you doing?' asked his mother.

'Eating Oliver Littlebody for breakfast,' mumbled the

red-necked schoolboy. 'I hate the skinny little runt. He's stealing my thunder!'

'It's those boots of his,' said his mother. 'There's something fishy about them.'

'Then I want a pair!' stamped the brattish boy wonder. 'It's not fair! I'm the best. He can't beat me!' But even though his father spent hundreds of thousands of pounds buying every pair of running shoes ever made, Anthony never found a pair like Ollie's, because Ollie had the only magic spikes in the world.

Come the day of the All England Schools Championship, Ollie was the clear favourite and he was quietly confident that Tommy Knock's shoes would steer him to victory. Anthony on the other hand was consumed by envy and loathing, and turned up at the stadium with a secret scheme to nobble his rival before the race. Winning was everything to Anthony, no matter how he achieved it!

Anthony had already changed into his running strip when Ollie and the old man appeared in the changing-room doorway. Anthony smiled as the antique coach pushed his skinny protégé forward.

'How lovely to see you, Oliver,' dissembled Anthony, turning on the charm like Jack the Ripper. 'By the way, congratulations on your results this year. You must have been training very hard.'

'He has,' said the old man. 'Now sit down Ollie and get changed. I'll wait for you out on the track.' The old man left the changing-room as Ollie sat down on the bench and unpacked his kit. Anthony stepped out of the shadows.

'Those must be your famous running shoes,' he said as Oliver produced Tommy Knock's spikes from his sports bag. 'May I have a look?'

'I'd rather you didn't,' said Oliver, clutching them tightly to his chest.

'Scared I might steal them?' laughed Anthony. 'Oliver really. I've got a brand new pair of my own. I'd hardly want to wear these smelly old things, would I?' And he snatched the boots out of Oliver's hands.

'No,' shouted Oliver, 'give them back!' but as he rose to reclaim them he was yanked back down by an invisible hand on the seat of his trousers.

'Problem?' enquired Anthony, slyly.

'I don't know,' trembled Ollie. 'I think my trousers are stuck to the bench.'

'Oh dear,' sympathised Anthony. 'I wonder how that happened?'

'Anthony, do something please. They're stuck to my legs as well. I can't take them off.'

'Well, I've got some glue if that's any help,' smirked Anthony, holding up a tube of Stik-Fast adhesive. 'On second thoughts it might just make matters worse.' Ollie's mouth fell open. Then bitter tears gave way to fury.

'You cheat!' he shouted. 'You've put superglue on the bench.'

'Only a little bit,' said Anthony. 'Now I really must go, I think I can hear the steward calling our race. Thanks for the spikes by the way. I think I might just try them out in the final if it's all the same to you.'

'No,' wailed Ollie as Anthony turned and left. 'NO! ANTHONY! DON'T LEAVE ME HERE!' But Anthony wasn't coming back.

Anthony cut a dash in his matching shorts and singlet as he ran out of the tunnel into the stadium. Tommy Knock's boots pinched him on the heel, but the roar of the crowd anaesthetised the pain and he bounced over to the stand where the girls were screaming for a stroke of his flowing, flaxen locks and bulging, brown thighs. While Anthony was having his ego rubbed, the old man was scouring the track for Ollie. There were only a couple of minutes left before the start of the race. Where was he? Then something made him glance down at Anthony's charcoal black running shoes.

The old man ran down the tunnel and into the long underground corridor that led to the changing-rooms. The tannoy was announcing the 400 metres final and he heard the crowd stamp its feet and cheer above his head. He found Ollie weeping on the bench.

'Why aren't you changed?' he bawled. 'What are you doing?'

'There's no point any more,' blubbed Ollie.

'I thought you wanted to beat Anthony more than

anything in the world,' said the old man. 'Now's your chance. You won't get another.'

'He's got Tommy's shoes!' Ollie wailed.

'Good!' exclaimed the old man. 'I was going to give them to him anyway. Now come on.' He yanked Ollie off the bench, tearing a huge, gaping hole in the back of the boy's trousers.

'What do you mean, you were going to give Tommy Knock's shoes to him anyway. Whose side are you on?'

'Trust me,' said the old man, pushing Ollie towards the exit, but the boy resisted. 'Look, Oliver you wouldn't have won if you'd worn those shoes today.'

'So what was all the training about?' gawped Ollie. 'You tricked me into doing your shopping for a year.'

'I made you believe you could beat him. And it's worked. You can! But you've got to run the race to do it.'

'Not without Tommy's spikes!' bellowed the bewildered boy. Why had the old man suddenly changed his tune? 'I want to win, not make a complete laughing stock of myself like last year.'

'Then get out there and compete,' shouted the old man. The tannoy was calling the runners to the track.

'No,' said Ollie. 'Not until you tell me why you've gone back on your word.'

'Magic is never straightforward, Oliver. What seems simple on the surface, often carries a hidden danger. If the boots can make you run like Tommy Knock, they can also make you die like him.' Ollie didn't understand.

'So how did he die?'

'After the race,' said the old man. 'Not get moving,' and he physically propelled Ollie out of the changing-room.

'But what about my kit?' squealed the boy.

'No time,' said his coach. 'You run as you are!'

Ollie stumbled out of the tunnel in his trousers and string vest. The crowd roared as he appeared, only this time with laughter as he tried to cover the hole in the seat of his pants.

'Ignore them,' said the old man. 'Concentrate on the race.'

'Please tell me why Anthony's got the spikes on,' begged Ollie for the last time.

'Because I knew Tommy Knock,' said the old man, mysteriously, and with that he pushed the small, barefoot boy on to the track.

Anthony St John Smythe smirked at Ollie as they knelt into their starting blocks.

'Thanks for the spikes,' he mocked. 'See you at the losing post!' Then the starter raised his arm and the crack of the starting pistol catapulted the runners from their blocks. Ollie rose with Anthony and entered the first bend on his shoulder, but Tommy Knock's magic spikes quickened Anthony's stride and pulled him away from the rest of the field. Ollie struggled to stay with him, but his legs were weak from no training and the harder he tried, the slower he ran. As Anthony accelerated into the final bend, Ollie threw an accusing look at the old man. No words were needed. Ollie hated his coach for making him look such a fool, and he hated him twice for standing there smiling and pointing up at the sky. It wasn't funny! Ollie could kill him! Up ahead, Anthony was surfing into the home straight, winning by a mile. Where was the old man's magic now?

Suddenly, the stadium shook to the deafening roar of a thousand throbbing prop engines. A dark cloud swept across the grandstand and plunged the track into shadow. Ollie looked up at the sky, expecting to see a squadron of low-flying aircraft, but there was nothing there; just the droning and the whistling. The high-pitched whistling that a bomb makes as it rushes to the ground. The old man was jumping up and down now, cheering. Anthony was twenty metres from the tape and Ollie was beaten . . . Or was he? The whistling stopped, the crowd fell silent and then with an almighty bang, an invisible bomb exploded on the track right in front of the lead runner. There was a white flash as Tommy Knock's running shoes were blown off Anthony's feet. They sizzled through the air like two flaming black crows and somersaulted back to earth beside a neat, pyramidic pile of St John's ashes. The race for first place was back on.

Ollie came seventh.

'So how did Tommy Knock die?' he asked the old man, after the medals had been presented and the ceremony of the Dustpan and Brush had swept Anthony St John Smythe off the track.

'In 1941, during the 440 final in the All England Schools Championship. He was hit on the head by a German bomb.'

'You mean, Anthony . . . ?'

'Blown to smithereens, Oliver. Copped a ghostly Luftwaffe whizzbang right between his ears.'

'Blimey,' gasped Ollie. 'That's powerful magic, that is.'

'It certainly is,' said the old man. 'It would have been you, if you'd been wearing the spikes.' Ollie gulped. 'Poor old Tommy Knock. We'll never see his like again.'

'What about me?' asked Ollie. The old man chuckled.

'I don't think so, Oliver. You'll never be a runner. You'll be a good chap, well worth knowing, the shopping proved that, but as for speed, I'd leave that to the tortoises from now on. They've got the edge.' The stringy boy grinned. He was pleased he didn't have to run any more.

'There is just one thing I'd like to know,' he said. 'Tommy Knock being blown up. He didn't suffer did he?' The old man took Ollie's hand and looked him straight in the eyes.

'The strange thing was,' he said, 'I didn't feel a thing.' Then he just disappeared in a puff of blue smoke, in much the same way as he'd disappeared fifty years before.

The Matchstick Girl

This is a sad sad story, concerning the life and death of Miss Polly Peach, born of poor parents in Victorian England. She had fifteen brothers and sisters and they slept eight to a bed. Boys to the right and girls to the left. Polly never went to school, but her mother and father did the best they could to instill a sense of right and wrong in their daughter.

'Stealing is bad,' said her dad.

'And working is good,' said her mum.

'But working for a boss who is stealing from you is bad,' said her dad. 'So you mind that don't happen to you.'

'You fight for what's yours,' said her mum.

'A fair wage for a fair day's work,' said her dad. And it was that type of chat that Polly Peach listened to every night before she went to bed.

On her eighth birthday she went out to work. The family needed her money, because her father had lost his job at the steel mill when they brought in them newfangled machines. There had been no money in the house for weeks, apart from the threepence ha'penny that her mother got for taking in washing. So Polly sneaked out, without telling a soul, and found a job as a matchstick girl, selling boxes of matches at the factory gates and down in the market square, where she stood on the foot of the statue of William Pitt so people could see her. And she sold well. On her first day, the owner of the matchstick shop congratulated her for selling twenty boxes of matches and paid her twopence. Polly was delighted and rushed home to her parents to present them with the money.

'You're a good girl,' said her dad.

'One of God's own,' wept her mum.

'But mind you're not stitched up like a haggis,' reminded her dad. And Polly remembered this every day for a week, when the owner of the matchstick shop paid her twopence for every twenty boxes of matches that she sold.

But one day, the owner changed the rules.

'Today,' he said. 'I'm paying a penny for twenty.'

'Why?' asked Polly. 'Am I not still working as hard as before?'

111

'Because I say so,' said the owner of the matchstick shop. 'And there's not a diddly squid you can do about it. Besides, the wife and I want a holiday in Blackpool, and we need every penny we can get.'

'But that's not fair,' argued Polly. 'My family needs that penny too.'

'If you're not happy with the job,' sneered the owner, imperiously, 'you know what you can do.'

'I do indeed,' said the little girl, remembering what her parents had taught her about standing up for her rights. 'I shall strike!' If only she'd known! If only poor, ignorant, dirty Polly Peach had known, that the one thing a matchstick girl should NEVER EVER do is strike. For no sooner had she uttered her threat, than there was a flash of phosphorescence and her head burst into flames. Before she could move, she was all fizzled out; just a thin, black, smoking stick with eyebrows.

The owner of the matchstick shop used Miss Polly Peach to winkle out the rough shag from his clap pipe, tossed her casually into an ashtray and went off to Blackpool for a fortnight with his wife, where (it grieves me to say) he had a most pleasing and restful vacation.

Simon Sulk

In a faraway place, at the northernmost tip of Iceland, but
a short snowball's throw from the Arctic Circle, lies a
tumbledown village by the name of Trollvik, where the
sun never shines and the ragged, pallid villagefolk wear
ghostly grey faces of stone that tell of their sorrow and fear.
For, as legend has it, Trollvik is home to the terrifying,
flesh-eating Trolls of the North.

A thousand years ago Trollvik was a prosperous fishing
port. One dark night, however, in the middle of winter,
the villagers were woken from their beds by a baleful
howling that split the night air like a woodchopper's axe.
Believing it was wolves, the elders gathered their people

inside the church and bolted the doors.

'We are safe in here,' said Thor their leader. 'The wolves cannot pass through stone walls.' But there was something unnatural about the howling that made him afraid. It sounded like the wolves were laughing at them. The villagers, however, trusted Thor and sang songs to drown out the baying. When it stopped, they cheered and toasted their leader for saving their lives. But when there was a knock at the door, they froze with fear.

'Who goes there?' bellowed Thor.

'Help,' came the pitiful reply. 'Help us please!'

'It is a trick,' whispered the elders to their leader. 'The wolves have disguised their voices! We mustn't let them in!'

'What do you want?' shouted Thor, cautiously.

'We are a family of gypsies,' was the desperate response. 'The wolves have attacked our caravan and dragged off our children. In the name of God, save us, before we are all killed.' Thor was unsure what to do. If he let these gypsies in and they *were* wolves, he would be condemning his people to certain slaughter, but if the gypsies were telling the truth . . . Just then, a flickering red light danced in the stained-glass windows of the church and the gypsies redoubled their cries. 'They have set fire to our caravan,' they wailed. 'We beseech you to let us in!'

'Open the doors!' commanded Thor. The villagers did as they were bid. When the bolts had been drawn back and the doors edged open, Thor saw, to his relief, a shabby family of travellers standing outside in the snow. But the flaming caravan was nowhere to be seen. Thor realised too late that he had been deceived, for just as he cried out, 'Beware!' the church doors were re-bolted and the gypsies were inside.

But they were not gypsies. Shedding their brightly coloured clothes and human shape, they transformed into a pack of snarling, slavering beasts. Wet-lipped, razor-toothed monsters from Beelzebub's bottomless pit, with powerful crushing jaws and matted fur that stank to high heaven.

'We are doomed!' wept the elders, as the villagers panicked and sought refuge behind the altar. 'They *are* wolves!'

'Not wolves,' snarled the leader of the beasts, as his soldiers surrounded the quaking crowd. 'We are much more powerful. Locked doors cannot keep our magic out.'

'What do you want?' asked Thor, bravely, pushing himself to the front.

'A home,' growled the leader. Then with a savagery unknown to the gentle people of Trollvik, the drooling demons butchered every man, woman and child, as they lay trapped within the desecrated church walls.

The beasts became known as trolls after the village that gave them a home. For five hundred years they terrorised the people from surrounding villages by snatching their children and roasting them over open fires like tender pieces of chicken. In the sixteenth century, King Magnus drove the trolls into the sea with a ten thousand strong army, but even today, Icelandic men and women still fear for the return of these homeless hounds from Hell.

But this is the stuff of mythology and, as we all know, trolls don't really exist. Not in Britain, anyway . . .

When Simon sulked, the whole street knew about it. He even woke the dead from their dusty sleep. Simon, you see, was a stamper, a ranter, a pouter and a shouter. If he didn't get his own way, he would barricade himself into his room until he did. One day, he got rather a nasty shock.

His mum and dad were moving to Devon, having sold their house to Mr and Mrs Thorsveldt, a nice couple from Rekjavik in Iceland. Simon had made it clear that he was not happy with the move. He didn't want to leave his friends at school and he liked the penny chews that he could buy at the shop on the corner of their street. His mum and dad explained to him that he'd make new friends in the country, but Simon shut out their commonsense by singing adverts at the top of his irritatingly flat voice. So it was hardly surprising that, when Simon's mum took her po-faced son to buy his new school uniform, Simon was less than co-operative with the lady in the shop.

'Puke!' he said. The lady smiled awkwardly.

'You look like a proper little gentleman,' she said to Simon.

'I look like a dustbin bag!' replied Simon, studying the reflection of his blazer in the mirror. 'I won't wear it!'

'He'll get used to it,' whispered the lady to Simon's mum.

'Well you would say that, wouldn't you, Miss Money-Grabbing-Greedy-Pants,' he grouched, 'because you just want to sell something, but I've got to wear it and I hate it!' He glowered at his mum with eyes as large as two polished bowling balls in a tub of vanilla ice-cream.

'Just pop it off Simon and let the nice lady pack it!' chirruped his mum, gaily, hoping to save the inevitable argument for home, but Simon never did as he was told. He sat down on the floor, thrust his hands in his pockets and pushed out his jaw till he looked like a grizzly bear. 'Come along dear, let's not make an ugly scene in the shop.' Simon's mum's forehead was beaded with sweat as customers poked their heads through the racked clothes to see what all the screaming was about. Simon had flung himself backwards across the display of sensible shoes and was kicking his legs in the air like a stranded beetle.

'I won't wear it. I'll spit and scream and throw up if you make me. I hate it more than I hate you. ALL of you! I don't want a smelly new uniform, I don't want to go to a ponky new school and I don't want to move house, so I won't!' That was telling them. The spectators looked away, tut-tutting beneath their precious flick-fringes, horrified that Simon's mum could produce such a sulky son in public.

When they got home, Simon's sulk was blacker than the Loch Ness Monster's liquid lair. His eyes had narrowed like arrow slits, his forehead had furrowed like a pair of grandpa Joe's baggy, corduroy, gardening trousers and his bottom lip was jutting out from his chin like the prow of an aircraft carrier. He stamped his spoilt feet on the hall rug and thumped upstairs like a bad-tempered baby rhino.

'You'll never see me again!' he bawled, as he slammed the door to his bedroom, and then, re-opening the door to throw his new uniform out on to the landing, 'I hope I die in here! Then you'll be sorry!'

Simon's mum and dad shared a despairing sigh as their son slammed his door for a second time and dislodged a trickle of plaster on to their heads. Then they returned to the depressing job of packing up their lives into tea-chests, before the removal men turned up at seven o'clock the following morning.

They were up at five. Simon was woken by the pitter patter of his parents' feet as they scurried up and down the stairs shouting orders to each other.

'Don't forget the loo seat. We're not a charity, you know,' said his dad.

'We can't take the loo seat, it's part of the house. Besides, what would the new owners sit on?'

'But it was me who bought it!'

'Yes and I bought the wallpaper, but we're not taking that with us, are we?'

'Should we leave the lightbulbs?'

'Oh, for goodness sake!' exploded Simon's mum. 'Why don't we just tear out the bricks and take the house with us.'

'Good idea,' bellowed Simon's dad, as he drifted into the garden to roll up the lawn.

Simon swung his legs out of bed and staggered over to the door. He was still half asleep. It was force of habit to go to the bathroom every morning before he got dressed. But just as he was about to turn the door handle, his mum cried out from the loft, 'Are you up yet, Simon?' and he remembered what he'd said the night before. Under no circumstances was he leaving his room if his parents were still hell-bent on moving house. He ran his tongue round his cacky mouth and sat back down on his bed. If his mum and dad wanted a fight, they could have one.

'SIMON?' His mum was still trying to rouse him. 'ARE YOU AWAKE?'

'No,' shouted Simon, 'I'm having a lie in.' He heard a metallic clatter as his mum descended the loft ladder at speed, then her voice on the other side of the door, soft and cajoling.

'Come on precious,' she whispered. 'You're not still angry with Mummy, are you? Look, it's a beautiful day. Come on out and we'll discuss your problem.'

'No problem,' said Simon, stubbornly, 'except with your hearing. I'm not leaving my bedroom and that's that.' Then, having said his piece, he crawled back under his sheets and stuck his pillow over his head.

All packing stopped. Simon's dad was called up from the garden where he'd been trying to uproot the sycamore tree, and both parents knelt outside their son's room, pleading with him to come out.

'It's no good sulking,' bristled his dad. 'You have to move house with us.'

'Can't make me,' replied Simon. 'In fact I'm going to hold my breath until you change your mind!' And his face turned crimson.

'I shall charge this door down if I have to,' threatened his dad.

'You won't get in,' screamed the purple boy, realising too late that he had just taken a breath. Then, hopping swiftly out of bed, he pushed a chest of drawers in front of the door, just in case his father was foolish enough to try any shoulder heroics. He could hear his mum sobbing, but he knew that she was only trying it on to weaken his spirit.

'Oh simple please, Mr Pieman,' she simpered. 'Boo hoo. Can't you hear how upset Mummy is? The removal men are due any minute.'

'Can't hear a thing,' chanted the boy, tunneling his fingers into his ears and la-la-ing at the top of his squeaky voice.

'Well, damn and blast you then!' shouted his dad, suddenly. 'You jolly well *can* stay there for all I care!' His temper had got the better of him, and he flounced down the stairs like a grand old knight of the theatre on hearing the news that his play was closing early.

Simon was still la-la-ing when the removal men lifted the tail-gate of their lorry and hopped into the cab.

'We'll see you in the new house, then,' said the foreman, doffing his baseball cap.

'We'll be right behind you,' shouted Simon's dad in a loud voice, designed to carry through Simon's window.

'You're not really going to leave him, are you?' begged his distraught wife. 'He is only ten years old.'

'Of course not,' explained Simon's dad. 'We'll pretend to leave with the removal van, so that he thinks we've gone, but really we'll be just round the corner having a cup of tea. When we sneak back, he'll be downstairs having breakfast and we can nab him.'

'He's our son, not a burglar,' said Simon's mum.

'You'll have to trust me on this one,' said Simon's dad. 'Besides what harm can come to him in half an hour?'

A couple of minutes later, Simon watched his parents drive away up the street without so much as a 'tutty-bye' or 'have a good life'. It would be foolish to pretend that he didn't view his isolation with a tinge of trepidation, but he'd guessed that they wouldn't really leave him. He was banking on them coming back, and when they did he'd make sure they didn't catch him. He was staying right where he was.

What Simon didn't know, however, is that *sometimes* being stuck behind a locked bedroom door is not the safest place to be.

A few minutes later, he heard a key fumble in the front door and beamed a smug smile to himself for successfully predicting his parents' feeble plan. The bare floorboards in the hall creaked as his mum and dad tiptoed towards the kitchen. Simon laughed. So, they *had* expected him to leave his room. He'd second-guessed their every move. He heard his father snarl when he discovered the empty kitchen and their impatient footsteps as they scuffled back into the hall. The staircase groaned as they crept upstairs. Did they think he couldn't hear? It was pathetic. They were outside his bedroom door now. They shuffled to a halt and then there was silence. Not just a quiet silence, but a silent silence. A long, heavy-duty pause, during which Simon became mesmerised by his own pulse rate. The longer it went on, the weightier it became, until at last Simon could bear the suspense no longer.

'So you came back, did you?' he mocked.

'We certainly did,' replied his mother's voice.

'Did we scare you?' asked his father.

'No,' said Simon. 'I knew you'd be back.'

'I meant just now, when we crept up the stairs?' whispered his father. His voice sounded strangely croaky like he had a cold. Simon bent down and put his eye up against the keyhole. It was his father all right, he'd recognise that horrible brown furry jumper anywhere.

'I'm not scared,' said Simon. 'And I'm not coming out either.'

'Oh dear,' said his mother, simply. 'Not even if I say please?' Simon heard a dog bark in one of the gardens that backed on to their house.

'I've told you a hundred times,' he said. 'I'm not coming out till you say we're not moving.'

'We're not moving,' said his father, quickly.

'Don't believe you,' said Simon. 'You must think I was born yesterday.'

'Simon dear,' came the soft tones of his mother, 'we want you out of the house now, do you understand?' Simon lay back on his bed and counted the lumps of Plasticene stuck on the ceiling. They'd have to do better than that. 'Mr and Mrs Thorsveldt are due any moment. What will they think if the house is still occupied?'

'What's that stink?' asked Simon, obliquely, twitching the end of his nose. 'It smells like the elephant house at London Zoo.'

'Unlock the door,' continued his mother.

'Has one of you stepped in dinosaur pooh, or something?' giggled the obstinate boy, as a second dog answered the first with a long baleful yowl. 'Even the dogs outside can smell it!' He was enjoying this conversation about dino do-do's so much that he failed to notice the change in his parents' tone. Gone were their calm requests, they were begging him now, with a desperation in their voices that was born of real danger.

'Help us,' whimpered his father. 'Save us, Simon. Let us in.'

'Save you from what?' he queried.

'The wolves,' sobbed his mother. 'The wolves are behind us. Their hot breath is on our backs.'

'Don't be stupid. They're dogs. They belong to the neighbours.' The howling had increased ten-fold. 'They're only household pets!'

'They're wolves!' screamed his mother.

'Wolves!' cried his father. 'In the name of God, save us, before we're both killed.' Simon was unsure of what to do. If he let his parents in and there were no wolves, he'd be in for a thorough pasting, but if his parents were telling the truth . . . Just then a flickering red light danced outside his bedroom window and his parents redoubled their cries. 'The house is on fire!' they wailed. 'Simon, we are your parents. We beseech you to let us in!'

Simon opened the door.

His parents were standing on the landing with tears streaming down their faces, but there was no fire. They pushed their way into the room and locked the door behind them.

'Very clever,' said Simon, sullenly. 'So, you've tricked

me. Well done. I suppose we'll be going to Devon now.' But even as he spoke, his parents were changing shape. Shedding their comfortable knitwear, they transformed into snarling, slavering hounds from Hell, with wet lips and razor teeth and matted fur that stank to high heaven.

'Who are you?' gasped the terrified boy.

'Trolls,' said the one who had been his mother.

'What do you want?'

'A new home,' they growled together. Then with three swipes of their powerful claws they tore Simon's head clean off the top of his petrified body.

Seconds later, the doorbell rang. Simon's parents had returned to pick up their son. The door was opened by Mr and Mrs Thorsveldt from Rekjavik.

'Hello,' they said in their faltering English.

'Have you seen Simon?' asked Simon's mum.

'No,' said Mrs Thorsveldt, with a look of concern in her bloodshot eyes. 'But you are most welcome to come inside to be looking for him.' And she opened the door to let Simon's parents cross the threshold, while Mr Thorsveldt smacked his lips and locked the door behind them.

Later that evening, Mr and Mrs Thorsveldt had a barbecue in the back garden, roasting succulent pieces of chicken (from three very large birds, I might add) over an open fire.

For all you know, they may be your new neighbours. Why don't you sniff 'em and see?

The Dumb Clucks

Once Upon a Time, in the Land of Stargazy Pie, wedged between the twin peaks of Mounts Feak and Weeble, in the forest-clad Welly-Wally Valley, there was a village called Dork. Dork was not like other villages because its villagers were all twits. And when I say twits, I mean real blockheaded boobies. These people believed anything that was told to them: 'The Earth is a spat-out piece of bubblegum on the hoof of a giant astral wildebeest.' 'Yum, scrum,' they would say, 'get chewing!' And they'd chew the earth half to bits before they realised that grass tasted disgusting and not like bubblegum at all. 'Ice cream cures the common cold.' So, during the winter months, they'd discard their woolly vests and smother themselves in frozen vanilla ice-cream. 'Well, it must be working,' they would say, 'because nobody gets colds any more.' Nobody got colds, because everyone was too busy croaking from double pneumonia. 'People who wear glasses are incredibly stupid.' Then why was it that when people removed their glasses to look wise they bumped into the furniture and walked over cliffs? Because they were boneheads, that's why. Gullible, thick-skulled ninnies, who believed whatever was said to them and never once stopped to ask why.

The worst of the villagers was a family called the Clucks. They were always the first to believe the latest gossip, the first to listen to superstitious claptrap, the first to set the family cat on fire to make their plums grow. They were staggeringly stupid. Believing that putting your clothes on inside out stopped your jeans from wearing into holes and eating a raw egg every morning stopped you turning into a chicken.

'Did you know,' announced Mr Cluck at breakfast one day, 'that sticking wasp stings into the soles of your feet is completely painless and makes your toenails grow.' The dumb Cluck children sat dumbly with their gawping gullets flopped open on their chests.

'Really?' said Mrs Cluck.

'Oh yes,' monotoned her halfwitted husband. 'I heard it on the radio, so it must be true.' Baby Cluck had stunned a wasp in her porridge. She pulled out the stinger and stuck it into her foot.

'Waaaaaaaaaaaah!' Her eyes exploded in gouts of tears as the pain shot through her leg and thumped into her shoulder.

'No, no,' said Mr Cluck. 'Tell her it doesn't hurt. It's good for her.'

'Stop it, baby,' demanded Mrs Cluck, 'your father says it doesn't hurt.' Well if Daddy said it didn't hurt, then it didn't, but baby Cluck could have sworn that her foot was throbbing like a belisha beacon.

One day, Dork suffered a terrible thunderstorm. Black clouds as thick as socks thundered overhead. Water gushed down the twin peaks of Feak and Weeble, converging in a swirling, muddy whirlpool in the middle of the market square. The local schoolteacher had it on good authority that things grew faster in the rain and stood his smallest pupils outside in the playground to soak up the water. After an hour he brought them back inside and declared his experiment a palpable success. His puny pupils had indeed grown, or at least their arms and legs were now sticking out of their jumpers and trousers. What he failed to realise was that the childrens' bodies had not grown an inch, it was just that their clothes had shrunk.

In the middle of the storm, a huge spike of lightning slashed across the sky, silhouetting a black figure on horseback at the end of the High Street. As he kicked his horse forward and moved into the village the rain stopped. By the time he was level with the school house, the sun was shining. Black horse, black boots, black moustache dangling from his top lip like a burnt worm. His clothes were torn and his hair was tangled like barbed wire.

The villagers were unused to cheroot-chewing strangers in their midst and rushed hither and thither, shouting, 'Welcome the stranger, welcome the stranger. How do we welcome the stranger?'

'Kick him,' came a tiny voice from the roof of the Dork Hotel. 'That's how to do it.'

'Don't be so stupid,' replied another. 'Guests should never be kicked. You should smother them in pig's grease and stick a feather up their nose!'

'Off with his head,' wailed a woman carrying a doughnut.

And a fourth voice shouted, 'Wait!' It was Mr Archibald Pojo, the cobbler. As the only sensible person in the village, he could always be relied upon to muster order out of chaos. Three generations of Dorks had learned to walk in a pair of Mr Pojo's no-nonsense, hardwearing, boat-like shoes. While the crowd waited to hear what Mr Pojo was going to say next, the stranger stopped in the market square. 'Let's ask him who he is,' suggested the cobbler.

'Ooh yes,' responded the crowd. 'What a brilliant idea! Hoorah for Mr Pojo! Who are you?' they shouted at the stranger, who was looping a revolver round his index finger.

His narrow-set eyes squinted as he spat a dollop of chewed red betel nut into the gutter and pushed his wide-brimmed black hat back off his forehead. His jaw was unshaven, like a nailbrush. Mr Cluck, his wife and their five-strong brood had slipped in next to the cobbler and were gazing gormlessly at the stranger, while he sucked his teeth and shifted his bottom lazily across his saddle.

'I'm the son of God!' he drawled, and everybody gasped. Mr Pojo laughed.

'That's a good one!' he said. 'And I'm Pope John Paul the Second!'

'Pleased to meet you,' said the traveller. 'I've brought a message from my dad.' Mr Pojo snorted at the ridiculousness of this cowboy's claims. Ambassadors from the Almighty usually had a touch of angel about them – wings and a halo, minimum – this man was tarred from top to toe with the Devil's slime. Any fool could see that . . . Mr Pojo surveyed the moony faces in the crowd . . . Any fool, but Mr Cluck and the rest of the Dorks. They were all cheering.

'Oh welcome, Son of God, who comes bearing a message from his dad!' shouted Mr Cluck. 'What are you doing here?'

'I've got a message of course,' said the stranger.

'Oh yes,' nodded Mr Cluck. 'So, what is it? It must be really important.'

'It is,' replied the cosmic cowboy, bluntly. 'The boss wants me to give you some good news.' There was an expectant buzz from the crowd. 'Now I won't tell you a lie, I CAN'T tell you a lie – that's one of the problems with being the son of God – so you'll just have to believe me when I say that dad has given me permission, for today and today only, to grant you all one wish!'

'Really?' blinked Mrs Cluck, excitedly. 'Any wish?'

'ANY wish.'

'I wish I had a hoverboard,' said Cluck Boy Number One.

'And I want a doll that spits,' added Daughter Number Two.

'Sssh!' hissed Mrs Cluck to her children. 'Don't be so greedy.' She turned her smile on the black-booted angel. 'Would God grant me a new set of hair curlers?' she enquired.

'Hair curlers? No problem,' said the divine being. 'God also does a nice line in electric blankets and toasters if any of you other ladies are interested.' Six hands shot up. 'See me after,' he winked, 'round the back.'

'Could God mend my golf clubs?' asked Mr Cluck.

'God will not only mend your golf clubs, but he'll chuck in six free golf balls as well!'

'Wow!' said Mr Cluck. 'I could get to like this God.'

'Well, that's the idea,' said his son. 'You see, he's coming down here in a few hours and he's looking for somewhere to stay.'

'Well, why doesn't he stay with us?' offered Mrs Cluck,

who was quite over-excited and silly about the prospect of owning new hair curlers. 'We could put the Z-bed up in the spare room, and we've got an extra blanket in the loft.'

'If you're sure. I know that Dad would love to stay with you. In fact, he was saying only the other day how much he wanted to meet the Cluck family.'

'Really?' beamed Mr Cluck.

'Oh, stop it!' giggled his wife. 'Now, you're making me blush!'

The village was bursting with communal pride. That God should have chosen Dork for a state visit was frankly unbelievable, but his son had said that he was coming and that was good enough for them. Mr Pojo, however, was not convinced.

'Look,' he explained to Mr and Mrs Cluck, 'I appreciate that having God as a house guest is a very great honour, but just suppose that this man is not a messenger from heaven at all, but a conman.' The Clucks gawped blankly. 'A liar,' simplified the cobbler. 'A thief.'

'Oh no, he definitely knows God,' protested Mr Cluck. 'He wouldn't be able to grant our wishes if he didn't.'

'Have you seen him grant any of your wishes?' retorted Mr Pojo, raising his voice so that others might heed his warning. 'Don't trust this man! Nobody pretends to grant wishes for nothing!'

'Killjoy!' shouted the crowd, and, 'Party-pooper!'

'Good people, believe me,' reassured the butter-wouldn't-melt-in-his-mouth-messenger, who had the mulish mob eating out of the palm of his hand, 'I'm here to give not to take. God is kind and generous and wants virtually nothing in return for granting your wishes.'

'So there is a catch!' triumphed the cobbler. 'You do want something.'

'Is smashing all the mirrors in Dork much of a price to pay for meeting God?' challenged the black cowboy. The crowd thought not. In fact they seemed to think it was a price well worth paying.

'Smashing mirrors!' exclaimed Mr Pojo. 'What has God to fear from mirrors?'

'He doesn't like to see his grisled face in the morning before he's shaved,' was the feeble reply.

'God has got a long white beard,' said Mr Pojo. 'Nobody will believe that.'

'I believe it,' piped up Mr Cluck. 'I don't like looking at my face in the morning, either.'

'Hear hear!' tub-thumped Mrs Cluck. 'Ra-ra!' went the crowd. And puff-puff went the self-important chest of Mr Cluck.

'Now go!' urged the messenger on horseback. 'Tear down your mirrors, fly to the boundaries of your village and splinter a girdle of broken glass round Dork!' The crowd cheered and dispersed like shrapnel exploding off a bomb, leaving Mr Pojo and the son of God facing each other across the market square.

'You don't fool me!' scoffed the cobbler. 'What are you up to?' The man in black struck a match across his beard and re-lit his cheroot.

'Wouldn't you just *love* to know,' he whispered.

When the crowd returned an hour later, having destroyed every mirror in Dork and scattered the glass round the village, they were as excitable as a bus-load of kids on a school outing.

'We've done it!' waved Mr Cluck, the buttons on his waistcoat popping with pride. 'You can call your dad and tell him we're ready for him now.'

'We've baked him some angel cakes as well,' announced Mrs Cluck, thrusting a plate of steaming, burnt buns under the messenger's nose. 'So he won't go hungry.'

'God never goes hungry,' smiled the cowboy, wickedly. 'Now there is just one more thing you must do before God will show his face.'

'Before you grant our wishes?' asked Mr Cluck.

'Exactly,' replied the messenger. Mr Pojo shook his head. This was it – the demand that would sell the villagers' souls to the Devil.

'God wants you to take off your shoes and burn them,' directed the stranger. The cobbler leapt to his feet.

'You can't burn my shoes!' he bellowed. 'What sort of messenger are you? Destroying my life's work to dupe these people! I won't let you do it, d'you hear!'

'God will not grant your wishes if you don't burn your

shoes,' threatened the heavenly messenger. 'We must all go barefoot before God as a sign of humility.' Mr Pojo turned to his fellow villagers and pleaded with their commonsense (what little they had).

'There is no God!' he shouted into a void. 'He is lying!' The crowd gasped, and the cobbler suddenly realised what he had just said. 'No, you misunderstand me. I meant that *his* God does not exist.' But the damage was done.

'Blasphemy!' roared the cowboy. 'Infidel! Take this disbeliever to the village walls and cast him out!' The mob surged forward and bore Mr Pojo to the outer reaches of the village, where they hurled him over the ring of broken mirror glass that now encircled Dork like a trail of glittering gunpowder.

The burning of the shoes was a splendidly roasty affair. The villagers danced barefoot round the bonfire and sang songs until the last of their soles had been consumed by the flames.

'Now what?' asked a sweating Mr Cluck. 'We've smashed our mirrors and burnt our shoes. It must be time to grant our wishes.'

'Nearly,' prevaricated the messenger, spitting blood-red betel nuts into the fire. 'God is almost ready to grant you your heart's desire, but he needs you to do one more thing for him first, just to prove that you love him.'

'Oh but we do,' blurted Mr Cluck, thinking largely of his new golf balls.

'Then you won't mind covering yourselves in mustard, will you?' said the cowboy, simply.

'I beg your pardon?' queried Mrs Cluck.

'Mustard or tomato ketchup, he likes both.' The Dorks were a little nonplussed by this remark. 'Or mayonnaise, if you prefer. What's the problem?'

'Oh no problem,' volunteered Mr Cluck. 'It's just that . . . why?'

'Why not?' asked the son of God, innocently.

'He's going to eat you,' came the tiny, far-away voice of Mr Pojo from the depths of the forest, but it was so tiny that only a fieldmouse heard it.

'Look, if you really must know,' sighed the cowboy, 'God's got a very sensitive nose. He cannot abide the stench of little people, which is why he asks you to cover up your smell with condiments and relishes.' He surveyed the sea of expressionless faces in front of him. Did the Dorks believe him or not?

'OK,' said Mr Cluck, accepting the cowboy's explanation with a cheery smile. 'I believe you. Break out the mustard!'

'Before you do,' interrupted the stranger, 'I must just check that Dad's in.' Then he removed a mobile telephone from his jacket pocket and punched in the numbers 666. 'Hello,' he said. 'Hello, is that God?' The village held its breath. 'They're ready for you now if you want to pop down . . . Yes . . . Yes . . . Yes, I understand. Ciao.' He

136

slotted the aerial back into its hole and grinned at the crowd. 'He'll be down in a jiffy,' he announced. 'Just feeding the Pit Bulls.'

Mr and Mrs Cluck were smearing ketchup behind their children's ears, when the first of God's heavy footsteps rumbled through the valley.

'Imagine us shaking hands with Deity!' squealed Mrs Cluck.

'Imagine us sharing toast with him at the breakfast table,' added her husband. 'Nobody will believe us. In fact, I can hardly believe it's happening myself!' The second footfall shook the ground and fractured the village water-pump, sending a spray of water high into the air. 'They won't be able to call us the dumb Clucks any more, will they, dear?'

'Certainly not,' said Mrs Cluck.

'English or French?'

'French please. It takes brains and vision to do what you've done today, Daddy Cluck.' The third footstep caused a minor earthquake underneath the clock tower, sending the big hand crashing to the ground like a thunderbolt from Heaven.

'That's right,' agreed Mr Cluck, tenderly plopping a glob of French mustard on to his wife's back. 'Today, we meet God, and tomorrow you can put your hair in curlers while I play a round of golf.' The fourth step had the crowd running for cover as a huge, cold, shadow swept across the square, and a large foot, the size of an ocean liner planted itself firmly on the top of Mount Weeble. 'He's big then,' stated Mr Cluck, who had no reason to believe that the ginormous black boot, ten times as high as the Empire State Building did not belong to God. Even when the one-eyed cyclops, with the pugilist's nose and stubbly beard thrust its ugly mug through the clouds, Mr Cluck was still in no doubt that he was staring at the face of Mr Infinite Beauty Himself. Only when the face split in half and revealed a stench of rotten teeth did Mr Cluck start to have his doubts. Only when the putrid breath rolled down the side of the mountain, like warm, gassy manure, did he turn to his wife with a quizzical look. Only when the fat, purple tongue smacked the fat, porky lips, did he ask himself if he had possibly been a touch too trusting of the cosmic cowboy and a mite too keen to dismiss Mr Pojo's warning. And only when the stomach belched and the knotted hand crammed the village church into the mouth, did Mr Cluck realise that he had been fooled. That this was not God, as the cowboy had promised, but an uncouth colossus with the table manners of an untrained warthog.

The giant tossed his straggly hair out of his eyes and roared with laughter. Spittle clung to his bottom lip and whirled round the Welly-Wally valley like a foaming Ferris wheel.

'YOU HAVE DONE WELL SON! I LIKE THE LOOK OF THIS PLACE AND I LIKE THE SMELL OF THESE OVEN-READY DORKS!' He sniffed in deeply and uprooted a couple of tall pine trees. They were sucked up by the draught and plugged his nostrils like two furry caterpillars.

'Excuse me,' enquired Mr Cluck's teeny-tiny voice underneath the giant's little toe, 'but where's God?'

'GOD?' queried the giant. 'NEVER HEARD OF HIM!'

'He's the most powerful being in the universe,' explained Mr Cluck, much to the admiration of his wife and children, who thought him extremely brave to be conversing with this gross freak of nature. In fact he was just plain stupid, but the two are often confused. The giant was becoming agitated.

'I'M GOING TO CHEW YOU IN HALF IF YOU DON'T SHUT UP!' he snapped.

'Why?' pushed Mr Cluck. 'Do you normally eat people?'

'I'LL GIVE YOU A CLUE,' chuckled the giant. 'MY NAME IS GIZZARD-GUZZLING, SINUS-SNAFFLING, OFFAL-OOMPHING, BONE-BREAK-ING, SKIN-SUCKING, FLESH-FLAYING, KIDNEY-CRUNCHING, BRAIN-BOILING, NECK-NIBBLING, LIVER-LICKING NIGEL!' There was a pause while Mr Cluck considered this.

'I had a cousin called Nigel once,' he said. 'He was a vegetarian.'

'WELL I **HATE** VEGETABLES!' bellowed the giant. 'GIVE ME RAW, DRIPPING FLESH ANY DAY OF THE WEEK.'

'I think what Dad's trying to say,' grinned the smug stranger on horseback, 'is that he's only here for one reason.

To woofle you all up like chocolate ants.'

'CRUNCH CRUNCH! THAT'S LUNCH!' slavered the unwashed man mountain.

'But you said he was God,' complained Mr Cluck. 'What about granting our wishes?'

'I lied!' ridiculed the man in black. 'My dad's never granted a wish in his life. You need a Fairy Godmother for that!' Then the giant smacked his beefy lips and tucked his handkerchief into the top of his shirt.

'RIGHT,' he drooled, with a glint in his single eye. 'WHO AM I GOING TO EAT FIRST?'

Now they may have been stupid, but the people of Dork could recognise a threat from a man-eating monster when it stared them in the face.

'Run!' shouted Mrs Cluck. 'He's gnashing this way!' But, of course, running was easier said than done, because none of them had any shoes on. And when they did reach the outskirts of Dork and could see the edge of the forest that would hide them from the great, guzzling giant, the villagers had to stop, because in their bare feet they could not cross the ring of broken glass that encircled the village. They had been gulled by their own greed. If only they had listened to Mr Pojo, who had recognised the cowboy's con trick and had realised that the stranger's promises of fame and fortune were worthless. But it was too late now. The cyclops's scheming son had locked the village with a bracelet of glass. He had trussed the villagers up good and tight, and had delivered them on a plate to his famished father, like butter-basted Christmas Turkeys.

Giant Nigel placed his chin upon the ground at one end of the village and opened his mouth.

'I'M A HOOVER!' he bellowed, sucking air through his teeth and moving his face slowly up the High Street. It was like a tornado in reverse. The villagers flew through the air like straws in the back-draught of a combine harvester, thumping into the giant's gums and sliding down his teeth on to his tongue. He was eating fifteen people in a single mouthful, crunching their bones like an anteater chomping termites. The Clucks had retreated into their coal cellar, hoping that Nigel would not find them, but as he hoovered closer, the entire house was sucked out of the ground leaving them exposed in a huddle.

'Oh dear!' whispered Mrs Cluck to her husband.

'What's the problem?' he enquired, glancing up to see a fifty foot nose sniffing their way.

'I've left the oven on,' she replied, 'with a souffle in. If I don't take it out soon, it'll be ruined.'

'Perhaps we could ask Nigel to turn the gas down,' suggested Mr Cluck, aware that the giant's mouth was now only three houses away, but marshmallow-brain Mrs Cluck couldn't make up her mind. 'I'll have to hurry you, Mummy Cluck,' prodded her witless husband, 'we're next on the menu!' But even as he spoke, the dumb Clucks were sucked into the giant's mouth, where they were licked, swilled, chewed and pasted, before being washed down with an extremely palatable vintage duck pond.

Dork was wiped off the face of the map. When Gizzard-guzzling, sinus-snaffling, offal-oomphing, bone-breaking, skin-sucking, flesh-flaying, kidney-crunching, brain-boiling, neck-nibbling, liver-licking Nigel had eaten his fill, there was not a building left standing, nor a tree, a human being, a dog or a blade of grass.

'DELICIOUS!' he burped. 'I'M STUFFED TO BURSTING!'

'Now then,' enquired his scheming son, 'where shall we go for supper?'

'I FANCY INDIAN TONIGHT,' said 'normous Nigel.

'Bombay it is then,' said the cosmic cowboy, and his father took one giant step to the right, and walked out of the Land of Stargazy Pie without showing his passport.

Nowadays in the Land of Stargazy Pie, wedged between the twin peaks of Mounts Feak and Weeble, in the forest-clad Welly-Wally Valley, there is a new village called Pojo. In contrast to Dork, it is full of the most questioning people in the world, people who refuse to believe what they are told, people who trust no one but themselves. In their own narrow way, of course, they are just as dumb as the people of Dork, but you try telling that to their founding father, Mr Pojo. He just won't believe you.

Doctor Moribundus

Such a sickly child was Lorelei Lee. Pale, paper cheeks, heavy-lidded eyes, stumbling gait and a waifish voice that squeaked most piteously when describing her ailments to parents and doctors alike. Oh, how she suffered, this poor, weakened child, how she bore her misfortune with stoical fortitude, how her sickness was never a problem to anyone else but herself. During *term* time, of course. In the school holidays, her powers of recovery were nothing short of miraculous.

Lorelei Lee was a shammer. She'd do anything to get out of going to school, short of actually cutting her nose off. In the middle of winter, she'd sleep with her head out of the window and her feet in a bucket of ice, in an attempt to catch cold. In summer she'd cover her neck and arms in honey to sweeten her flesh for the mosquitoes, so that they'd bite her and give her malaria. She'd eat secret bowlfuls of jam and sticky cakes in her bedroom to bring up spots, and she'd lie for hours in the bath till her skin dried out and flaked off in chunks.

'What is it?' her mother would shriek.

'Leprosy,' Lorelei Lee would reply. 'And I was so looking forward to school today!' She'd stick plasters all over her body and savagely rip them off, leaving ugly red welts underneath.

'It's the plague!' wailed her mother and Lorelei Lee had another three days in her bed. She'd press a freezing wet flannel to her forehead to simulate cold sweats, eat curried chilies at midnight to raise a fever, and slip live money-spiders down the back of her throat to give herself a really effective tickly cough. On the days when she had nothing blotchy or phlegmy to show her mother, she'd feign dizziness or stomach cramps and claim to have a temperature. When her mother brought the thermometer, Lorelei Lee would stir her cup of tea with it or stick it on top of the radiator before slipping it under her tongue.

'108!' her mother would shriek, or '112!' People were supposed to die at 104. Her mother would go into a windmill flap, knocking pictures off the wall in her haste to reach the telephone and call out the doctor. And Lorelei

Lee would secure another twenty-four hour bunk off from school.

Every morning was the same. Once Lorelei Lee had tricked her mother into letting her stay home, with a performance of feeble moans and feigned gasps of pain, the wan little girl would rally sufficiently to enjoy a large breakfast of two boiled eggs and six slices of buttered toasty soldiers.

'Are you sure you can manage all that?' her mother would ask, concernedly.

'I'll try,' Lorelei Lee would tremble, coughing softly into her duvet, 'and I'll try to go to school tomorrow. I promise. You know how much I *hate* to be ill.'

'Now, you just lie back and get better,' her mother would say. Then she'd run down to the shops (while Lorelei Lee trampolined on her bed) and buy fifteen different comics, a dozen puzzle books and a large bar of nutty chocolate, because that was Lorelei Lee's favourite. The rest of the day alternated between telly-watching and watching the telly. She sat up in bed and channel-hopped until her mother carried up her next meal, whereupon, hearing her mother's footsteps on the landing, she would ease herself under the covers and pretend that she had just woken up and was feeling a *little bit* better, but still couldn't tell how she was going to be tomorrow. Come nighttime, however, when her father returned from the office, Lorelei Lee would jump out of bed and declare herself perfectly cured and raring to go. Every night, you see, her father would return home with a get-well present for his delicate princess – a bow for her pretty head, a pair of silk stockings or a nursey-nursey doll to take care of her while he was away.

It has to be said that the doctors who attended Lorelei Lee's sick bed were a useless bunch. Overworked and under-her-thumb, they flitted in and out of her bedroom like gadflies, pausing just long enough to take her pulse and tap three fingers on her back. To a man and woman they declared themselves baffled by her illnesses. They hadn't a clue what was wrong with her, but happily wrote out the prescriptions that Lorelei Lee demanded; deliciously sweet blackcurrant pastilles for her permanently sore throat, soothing tiger balm for her fevered brow, and a dozen acacia honey milkshakes – the sort most people use for slimming, but which Lorelei Lee just happened to like rather a lot.

One day, however, Lorelei Lee went too far. The sun was shining as she got out of bed. She'd never felt better in her life, but she had Latin at school before break and she hated dead languages. A spectacular disease was called for. As she stood at the sink, brushing her teeth, she had an idea. Hearing Lorelei Lee's distressed cries, her mother took the stairs five at a time. She burst into the bedroom to see her daughter lying on the floor, shaking like a jelly and foaming at the mouth – a huge, white waterfall of foam, cascading over her lips and dribbling down her chin on to the carpet.

'What is it? What is it? What is it?' screamed her apoplectic mother. 'Are you ill, Lorelei Lee?'

'I fear that I am,' trembled Lorelei Lee's lathering larynx.

'Are you going to *die*?' blurted her mother.

'Let's put it like this, I wouldn't bother cooking me lunch,' groaned Lorelei Lee, dramatically, checking to see how her performance was going down. Her mother was kneeling on the floor with her head propped against the end of the bed, blubbing like a two stroke lawnmower. 'I think I've got rabies,' announced Lorelei Lee. Rabies! The word sank into her mother's heart like a mad dog's tooth!

'Rabies,' she gasped. 'That's a serious one, isn't it?' Lorelei Lee nodded her head.

'Worth at least two days off school, I'd say,' she said.

'I must get a specialist before you turn into a werewolf!' howled her mother as she sprinted out of the bedroom and clattered down the stairs to the phone. Lorelei Lee wiped the toothpaste off her chin and grinned. What a sensational actress she was.

Fifteen minutes later, there was a screech of brakes in the street outside. Lorelei Lee looked out of her window and saw a smartly dressed man carrying a briefcase step out of a chauffeur driven Rolls Royce. He was met at the gate by her mother and ushered inside. As they climbed the stairs, Lorelei Lee touched up her foam and hopped into bed. When her mother entered the room with the be-suited gentleman, Lorelei Lee was lying quite still, as stiff as a corpse, staring up at the ceiling like a stuffed fox with glass eyes.

'This is Dr Nick,' said her mother, with lips that fluttered from fear and mental anguish. 'He's from the government, Lorelei Lee. He wants to ask you some questions.' Lorelei Lee concentrated hard on the light fitting to stop herself from blinking.

'Hello,' said Dr Nick, sitting down on the bed and placing his hand on her forehead. 'I'm the world's foremost expert on rabies.' A foremost expert! Lorelei Lee gulped. 'How are we feeling?' She didn't answer. She just kept staring. 'Are we hot?' She nodded. 'That's strange, because your forehead's stone cold. How's the pulse?' he enquired, picking up her wrist with two fingers and a thumb. He counted to thirty. 'Nothing wrong there.' Then he dipped his long finger into the puddle of foam on Lorelei Lee's duvet and licked it with the tip of his tongue. 'Hmmm,' he noted with surprise, 'peppermint. And when did the foaming start? Before or after you cleaned your teeth?' Lorelei Lee closed her eyes and pretended to faint, so she wouldn't have to answer any more tricky questions. He was dead smart this doctor. Not like the others. Fortunately, Lorelei Lee's mother flipped her lid at precisely this moment, distracting the doctor's attention from her daughter's despicable deception.

'Is my precious angel going to live?' she bawled.

'Your precious angel,' said the doctor grimly, swallowing each word like a bitter pill, 'will survive.' Then he muttered under his breath. 'More's the pity.' He was a busy man and didn't like having his time wasted.

'But should I send her to school?'

'Not until she's had my prescription,' he ordered, flatly, scribbling a quick note, which he handed to Lorelei Lee's mother. 'See to it that she takes this tonight, once and once only. Twice will kill her.'

'And this will cure her of the rabies?'

'My dear lady,' replied the tall doctor, backing out of the room, like an undertaker at a funeral retiring from the coffin, 'it will cure her of a whole lot more than that.'

Lorelei Lee opened an eye and wondered what he meant.

The strange thing was that even though Lorelei Lee's mother went to six different chemists, none of them had ever heard of Dr Nick's prescription.

'Nobody knows what this *Medicus Moribundus* is,' she panicked, when her husband got home from work that night, 'and Dr Nick specifically said that Lorelei Lee was to take it tonight.'

'How is she now?' he asked.

'Oh much better,' she replied. 'She was a bit off colour after Dr Nick left, hardly touched her breakfast, but she had three helpings at lunch and she's upstairs now eating her supper in front of the telly.'

'Then there's nothing to worry about, is there?' comforted Lorelei Lee's father. 'We don't need Dr Nick's prescription if she's got rid of the rabies on her own.'

Just then, the doorbell rang. A long, haunting chime that only ceased when Lorelei Lee's father slid open the door. Standing on the doorstep was a fat woman dressed in a bulging, black uniform. She had a patch over one eye and a wild thatch of hair that sat on the top of her head like a gorse bush. She was carrying a Gladstone bag and presenting a calling card for Lorelei Lee's father to take.

'At your sssservice!' she lisped, spraying the hall with her spittle. 'Go on, take the card, it won't bite!'

'I'm sorry?' puzzled Lorelei Lee's father. 'Who did you say you were?'

'Oh ssssilly me!' slobbered the fat black lady. 'I forgot. I am the night nurse, assistant to the world famoussss healer and medicine man, Doctor Moribundus! You ssssent for ussss!' If she slobbered much more, Lorelei Lee's father would need to put his anorak on.

'Who is it?' called out Lorelei Lee's mother from the kitchen.

'A Dr Moribundus,' replied her husband. 'What do you want?' he asked, turning back to the night nurse, but the slavering stranger was no longer there. In her place was a tall black pillar. A man in a black cape and jack boots. A man with curly black painted fingernails. A man with a thin black beard down the centre of his chin like a duelling scar. A man with long black hair beneath a wide-brimmed hat. A man with cold black eyes. A man (or so Lorelei Lee's father suspected) with a heart as black as the long, dark night before God shone His torch on the world.

'Good evening,' said Dr Moribundus. 'We've come to see Lorelei Lee.'

'Did you say Dr Moribundus?' said Lorelei Lee's mother, excitedly, coming through from the kitchen. 'That's what *Medicus Moribundus* must mean. Have you come with Lorelei Lee's prescription?'

'No madam,' said the shadowy figure. 'I *am* Lorelei Lee's prescription. Now if it please you, I would see the patient now.' He took a stride through the door and stood in the middle of the hall. His nose twitched. 'Ah yes,' he sniffed, 'I can smell her. Upstairs quickly nurse. We have precious little time if we are to save the poor soul.' Lorelei Lee's mother gasped.

'You mean, my beautiful baby might die?'

'She is not a well child,' said the doctor. 'Her frequent absence from school would indicate a weak constitution. Under such circumstances, I always advise parents to prepare for the worst.'

'Oh!' Lorelei Lee's mother swooned into her husband's arms.

'But we will do what we can for her. Come nurse, away!'

'Shouldn't we be there?' panicked Lorelei Lee's father. 'Can't we help?'

'In cases as serious as this, sir, 'tis best I work alone, but I must warn you not to interrupt my labours. No matter what you hear, for there *will* be screams, you must not enter the bedroom. Lorelei Lee's salvation rests in my hands alone. Now I must to work for there is much to be done!' Dr Moribundus swept up the stairs, trailing his billowing cape like a vulture's wings, while Lorelei Lee's mother and father stood in the hall like a couple of prunes at a plum wedding.

Lorelei Lee was watching *Peak Practice* when the doctor and his assistant burst into the room.

'Curtains,' ordered Dr Moribundus, locking the door behind him. 'And switch that television off.'

'Who are you?' snapped Lorelei Lee. 'Get out of my bedroom!' The doctor threw off his cape and pulled her dressing-table over to the side of the bed.

'Shut up,' he said, 'or I'll tear out your tongue. I'm a doctor. You can trust me.' Lorelei Lee cowered back on to her pillow as the night nurse unpacked the doctor's bag on to the dressing-table, laying out his medicines and surgical instruments in neat little rows. 'I hear you've not been well,' said the doctor, snapping a pair of rubber gloves on to his hands.

'So what's been the problem?' he asked, removing the lid off a jarful of leeches.

'Nothing,' exclaimed Lorelei Lee. 'I'm fine.'

'That's not what the school register says,' said Dr

Moribundus. 'Roll her over, please nurse.'

'No really, I'm much better,' squealed Lorelei Lee, as the night nurse tumbled her roughly on to her back and pinned down her arms.

'Blood-letting,' said the doctor, attaching a dozen leeches to the shaking girl's neck and arms, 'purifies the system better than anything else I know.'

'Ow! They're biting!' squeaked Lorelei Lee.

'They're leeches, my dear. They're meant to.'

'They've only just sssstarted!' cackled the night nurse. 'Wait till they ssssuck you dry!' Lorelei Lee could feel the leeches slithering behind her ears. She screamed.

'The patient is hysterical,' said the nurse. 'Shall I prepare the calming mussstard poultice, doctor?' Dr Moribundus nodded his head.

'Smear it all over,' he instructed his assistant.

'Will it hurt?' wailed Lorelei Lee.

'I hope so,' smiled the doctor. 'No pain, no gain!'

Downstairs, Lorelei Lee's parents sat in silence listening to their daughter's screams and did nothing. They were following doctor's orders.

'You see,' smiled Dr Moribundus, as the nurse unwrapped the host mustard poultice from the girl's blistered skin. 'I believe in the powers of alternative medicine. What we have here is a severe case of Noschoolitis, and you know what that means, nurse.' The assistant rubbed her podgy hands together gleefully.

'Sssssnip ssssnip!' she snickered.

'Brain surgery!' pronounced Dr Moribundus.

'Brain surgery!' yelped Lorelei Lee. 'But brain surgery's not an alternative medicine.'

'It is the way I do it,' leered Dr Moribundus, with a sparkle in his eye.

'I'm cured!' shrieked Lorelei Lee, sitting up on her bed.

'Not yet, but you will be,' retorted the doctor. 'Scrub up and sterilise, nurse!'

'But I'm OK now. I'm as fit as a flea,' begged the quivering girl.

'Now this might hurt a little bit,' said the doctor, testing the sharpness of his scalpel by opening a vein in his finger, 'but when the operation is over, I guarantee you won't have another day's illness in your life.'

'I will go to school,' pleaded Lorelei Lee. 'Every day, just you see!'

'Too late for that now,' said Dr Moribundus. 'Nurse?'

'Yesss.'

'The needle.' It was five feet long, like a javelin. The nurse produced it from Dr Moribundus's black bag like a sword from a scabbard. The steel shaft glinted as he tapped out the air bubbles inside the syringe and squeezed the plunger. Lorelei Lee whimpered as the night nurse dragged her to her feet.

'But I haven't got rabies!' she cried. 'I don't need an injection!'

'I know,' said the doctor, leaping on to the bed and plunging the needle into the top of her skull. He pushed down hard until it poked out the bottom of her feet. She was skewered to the floor like a lump of kebab meat, pinned by a steel spine running from her head to her toe, muted by a silver bodkin through her tongue. Only her wide eyes, standing proud like two vaselined golf balls, gave any hint of her fear. Dr Moribundus picked up a saw. With three powerful strokes he sliced off the top of her head and flipped back the lid to expose her brain.

'Comfortable?' he asked. The nurse handed him a teaspoon. He dipped it into Lorelei Lee's skull, flicked out the bad bit in her brain that made her feign illness, and ate it, just as you or I would eat a soft boiled egg.

When Lorelei Lee awoke in the morning, she was glowing with health. She was in the pinkest of pinks and looking forward to school. From then on, she never had another day's illness in her life. Even when she caught a cold, she kept it a secret, just in case Dr Moribundus paid her another visit in the middle of the night. She missed school only once again, when the top of her head mysteriously flipped open in a gale, but she was only absent for a morning while they stapled the two halves back together. By twelve o'clock she was back in class being tested on her Latin vocabulary.

'Can anyone tell me what *Medicus Moribundus* means?' asked the teacher. 'Yes, Lorelei Lee?'

'Ith it a big plunging needle?' she lisped through the hole in her tongue. The teacher laughed, scratching the thin black beard down the centre of his chin.

'Now I wonder what gave you that idea?' he said.

Needles to say, Lorelei Lee didn't tell him.

The Stick Men

You've never heard of The Stick Men? Pencil-thin people with leaded bones and huge round heads like pumpkins? Mad staring eyes on their foreheads and cheeks, sliced melon smiles with ranks of tombstone teeth, jug handle ears, unjointed limbs and six strands of wavy hair wiggling out of their scalps like sun-seeking worms? You must've seen them. Look in your school books. It's you who creates them.

From the beginning it was the fault of Chico's parents for putting his cot too near the wall. What did they expect a child of eighteen months to do if they put him to bed with a pack of felt pens and a sheet of clean wallpaper? At first it was just scribbles, abstract doodles produced for the fun of mixing colours and the squeaky noise that the pens made if he pressed really hard, but as he grew older, Chico moved on to things and people, because things and people could talk to him.

Chico was the only child of not-now-can't-you-see-I'm-working-parents, farmed out to a continuous stream of TV-watching, fridge-raiding, boyfriend-phoning nannies, who loved being alone in the house all day, but didn't much care for the child caring bit. They never took Chico out to meet children of his own age and as a result he grew up alone, creating his friends with a crayon. They were all scribbled stick men, of course, with n-shaped legs and crucifix arms and heads like beach-balls.

His parents didn't approve. Chico's mother was always 'must fly-ing' to work, but whenever she did visit her son she always had a fit.

'Look at my expensive silk wallpaper!' she wailed. 'How could you scrawl such ugly people all over it?'

'They're not ugly,' said Chico. He pointed to a long-legged stick lady with candyfloss hair. 'That woman's a supermodel. She's beautiful.'

'You vandal!' ranted his mother. Her pearl necklace clattered against her neckbone as she thrust her nose into Chico's face. 'Have you got a brain inside that head of yours?'

'We were having lunch,' explained Chico, indicating

his drawing of a rickety wooden table laden with sausages and surrounded by guests. 'Mr Wells, the Waterboard Man was there, along with Tammy and Crispin and that new boy in number forty-seven . . . oh what's his name? . . . Gregor, that's it. His father's a butcher, so I asked the farmer to join us, but of course he *never* comes to lunch unless he's got his entire farm with him, so that meant pigs and sheep and Henry Horse and the new ducklings who only hatched out last week, and they all made such a row that the policeman popped in to see what was going on and stayed for a slice of banoffi pie – it's his favourite, see – and one thing led to another and suddenly it was way past everyone's bedtime and I had to call a taxi to take them home, but the taxi got a puncture and that's why there's an AA van outside my house.' Chico pointed to a yellow splodge with wheels on. 'It was quite a do, actually. You should have been there.' His mother's face had turned purple.

'You're insane,' she gasped. 'These scribblings aren't real. You need to see a doctor.'

'I'm just making friends,' he mumbled, twisting the cord on his pyjama bottoms.

'Not on my new wallpaper you're not!' she bawled, tripping to the door in a high-heeled fluster and screeching for Chico's father, who was interfacing his modem with Manhattan and did not take kindly to being disturbed. He had a face like erupting Vesuvius when he came through the door and a voice like a foghorn.

'Explain this interruption!' he roared.

'I'm sorry dear, but Whatsisname's been drawing on the walls again,' sneaked Chico's mother.

'Whatsisname who?' he quivered.

'Your son, Chico. That thing over there,' she clarified.

'Oh him,' sneered Chico's father. 'Is he still here? I thought we'd decided to put him out with the rubbish months ago. How tedious. I'm stopping your pocket-money, boy!'

'You don't give me pocket-money,' said Chico.

'Don't I?' said his father. 'Well, remind me never to start then! Confined to your room for two days!' Just then his mobile phone rang. 'Yes?' he barked. 'Right. That's a deal.' He snapped the aerial back and turned to his wife. 'That was Mrs Cook. Breakfast's ready.' Then they turned on their Gucci heels and marched downstairs without so much as a backward glance.

That was the last time Chico's parents ever saw their son. Had they known, I daresay they might have shaken him by the hand and wished him well, maybe even pecked him on the cheek, but there again, maybe not. They'd never really enjoyed Chico, never seen the point of him. If he'd been born a kettle, they'd have taken him back to the shop and exchanged him for something more useful, like a toasted sandwich maker. At least a toasted sandwich maker can make toasted sandwiches. Chico can't.

The Stick Men

His mother and father had long since left for work (in separate private helicopters), when Nanny Sharon arrived at the house. She was twenty minutes late and in something of a hurry to phone her boyfriend to let him know that she'd got there safely. Chico slid his crayons out from underneath his bed and pondered where to go that day. He could draw himself a visit to the fire station and rescue a family from a burning barn, or go to the seaside and share his tuna fish sandwich with the 'M-W' seagulls, or go to a football match and watch Arsenal play football for once. Even the impossible was possible in Chico's world. But no, he would pay a visit to the enchanted forest of Fiddledy-dee. Chico had started to draw this scene once before, back in March, but had been interrupted by the arrival of his grandmother armed with an Argos catalogue, wanting to discuss family Christmas presents. Ever since that day Chico had longed to return to the enchanted forest, but had never found the time. He wanted to explore its shadowy caves (where the knobbly hobgoblins roasted lizards over an open fire), to visit the sorceress's castle at the top of the hill, and to pick the giant toadstools that grew as tall as totem poles on the banks of the magic river. It was a place where any-thing could happen, just as long as Chico could draw it.

Nanny Sharon was yabbering on the phone downstairs like a lovesick monkey, so Chico knew he wouldn't be disturbed. He selected an empty space on the wallpaper and as he sketched, imagined himself inside his picture.

It was a hot summer's day and the enchanted forest was sweet with birdsong. The clear blue waters of the magic river twinkled through the trees. Plump little children splashed in the crystal rock pools and climbed the giant toadstools, playing crow's-nest lookout for their pirate mates below. Smiling parents laid picnic rugs on the lush green grass and prepared chicken mayonnaise sandwiches and strawberries with cream. Mums in flowing flowery dresses, dads with rolled up sleeves and thick brown forearms. The sorceress's castle gleamed like a star on the top of the hill and outside the open drawbridge in a field of buttercups sat the sorceress herself in a rainbow-coloured deckchair, performing magic tricks for a group of wide-eyed children; turning sand into gold and tears into diamond-drops.

That's how it was in his head, but not on paper.

There was a knock on Chico's bedroom door. It was Nanny Sharon with lunch; a curly-cornered, cowcumber sandwich.

'What'ch'ya doin' then?' she drawled in nasal Essex-speak. 'Don'ch'ya never do nuffin' but all that paintin' 'n' that? Mad you are, Chico. Stark starin' bloomin' bonkers.' She was sneering at his mural. 'It's a bloomin' mess 'n' all. Call that a pikchure? I got a free year old niece could do betterer 'n' that!'

'It's the enchanted forest of Fiddledy-dee,' explained Chico. 'I've got friends there,' and he pointed out the stick men.

'Bloomin' weird friends,' cackled Nanny Sharon. ''eads like punch bags, bodies like lolly sticks! I wouldn't want one of them kissin' me down the Roxy on a Saturday night! 'E might slip darn me froat!' She laughed like a non-starting car on a cold winter morning.

When she had gone Chico saw his picture differently. He saw it the way Nanny Sharon had seen it, *without* the magic. In his imagination, the sorceress's castle had stood tall and straight with flag-waving turrets at each corner. In the picture, the castle tilted to the right, squidged out in the middle like an overfilled sponge cake and fell down the hill to one side. The enchanted forest was more of a copse and the hobgoblins' heads were so huge and bulging with warts that they didn't fit through the entrance to their cave. The magic river looked more like a puddle, the giant toadstools like street lamps (with long thin stalks and pin-prick heads) and the sorceress was blind, because Chico had forgotten to give her any eyes. Fiddledy-dee was an ugly, barren world, full of scribbles and splodges and spud-headed stick men.

'So?' said a teeny tiny voice down by Chico's shoe. 'What's wrong with spud-heads?'

'I beg your pardon?' said Chico, wondering where the voice had come from. It wasn't inside his head, but something small and boney was crawling up his leg. 'Who is this?' he squeaked, nervously.

'In your lap,' replied the shrill voice. Chico looked down

and there, clambering over the buckle on his belt was a real stick man. Chico screamed.

'Well don't be like that,' said the matchstick cartoon. 'I can't help looking the way I do. *You* drew me!' He had a huge circular head that lolled around on top of his coat-hanger shoulders like a heavy cannonball. 'Mind if I lie down?' he sighed, resting his spindly legs in the palm of Chico's hand, 'only it's hard work lugging this vast nut round all day.'

'Sorry,' said Chico. 'I'm not very good at drawing.'

'Not very good!' sneered the stick man. 'You're ruddy useless.'

'Yes, all right!' snapped Chico, who was feeling a little sensitive about his art since Nanny Sharon's blunt criticism. 'What are you doing here?'

'The sorceress sent me. Name's Stan, by the way. She wants to meet you, wants to thank you for bringing Fiddledy-dee to life.'

'All of it?' gasped Chico. 'How?'

'It's enchanted, isn't it? Magic, I suppose.'

'Real magic?' asked Chico. Stan nodded his outsize, dinner-plate head and toppled over from the weight of it.

'Look, I shouldn't be asking,' he asked, as he picked himself up, 'but it's dead boring standing stock still on a wall all day, and my mates were wondering if we could let our hair down for five minutes?'

'What do you mean?' puzzled Chico.

'Can they come out of the picture and have a bit of fun in your bedroom?'

'Yes please,' beamed the lonely boy. He was dying to meet his drawings.

'Word of warning, though,' added Stan sternly. 'Whatever you do, don't invite the knobbly hobgoblins. They'll just get over excited and silly.'

Then, with one clap of Stan's hands the bedroom wall became a flurry of black pencil lines and the carpet seethed with bulbous-headed stick men of all shapes and sizes.

'So what sort of fun did you have in mind?' asked Chico.

'Scribbling,' grinned Stan mischievously and before Chico could call a halt, the stick men had grabbed a crayon each and had covered his bedroom in streaks of red, whirlpools of blue and split-splats of green and magenta.

'My parents will kill me!' he wailed, as the mess spread up the walls like rising damp. 'Stop it, this instant!'

'Ssh!' hissed Stan, 'keep your voice down or you'll wake the hobgoblins!' But his warning came too late.

'What do you care if you upset your parents?' growled a deep-booted voice behind Chico's shoulder. He turned round to see Impey, the hobgoblin's leader, posing with his gang in front of the skirting-board. They may only have been two inches tall, but the hobgoblins were a fierce looking bunch. Scowling faces, warty necks and broken, brown teeth from crunching too many lizards. 'Want to see some black magic?' he leered.

'Oh dear, I knew this would happen,' fussed Stan. 'Don't let them do it, Chico.'

'Do what?' asked the boy.

'This!' roared the hobgoblin leader, snatching a crayon off the floor and sketching a brilliant cartoon of Nanny Sharon talking on the phone.

'That's an amazing likeness,' gasped Chico.

'It's not finished yet,' sniggered Impey. The stick men held their heads in their hands as Impey added a snake to his drawing; a long, slithery, silver serpent with a red forked tongue, sliding out of the ear piece of Nanny Sharon's telephone.

There was a blood-curdling scream from downstairs as Nanny Sharon dropped the phone. Seconds later, the front door slammed and she was gone.

'You didn't . . .' gasped Chico.

'I did,' chortled Impey. 'A snake in the ear always get 'em. Want to see another?' Before Chico could stop him, he'd scribbled two helicopters on the bedroom wall.

'No,' shouted Chico. 'You're not allowed to hurt my parents!'

'Why not?' laughed the hobgoblin. 'They don't care about you,' and he finished his picture with a flourish. Only when he withdrew his hand did Chico realise what he'd drawn. The two sets of rotor blades had clashed in mid-air and the helicopters were crashing. Chico grabbed the rubber off his desk and herded the hobgoblins back towards the wall.

'Get back in the picture!' he ordered. 'That's a wicked thing to draw.'

'It's only a bit of fun,' protested Impey.

'It's sick,' shouted Chico, rubbing out the helicopter crash and shooing the hobgoblins back into their caves.

'I did warn you,' sighed Stan. 'There's nothing a hobgoblin likes more than a bit of mindless violence.'

'Well, there's no room for yobs like that in Fiddledy-dee,' stated Chico, rubbing the hobgoblins out of his picture. 'The enchanted forest is a smiley place where the sun shines. I made a mistake. They don't fit in.'

'Talking of sunshine, shall we go see the sorceress now?' asked Stan.

'Yes,' said Chico, 'but how do I enter the picture?' The stick man raised his thick, pencil eyebrows and sighed.

'You draw yourself in, of course!'

When Chico arrived in the picture and surveyed all that he had drawn, he got a rude shock. Now that it had come to life, he was expecting the enchanted forest to match the perfect picture in his mind. Unfortunately, it matched the scrotty picture on his wall. There were no plump little children splashing around in crystal rock pools, just stick men floating on a puddle. There were no pirate games up and down the giant toadstools, just stick men stuck up lamp posts. There were no pretty mums and practical dads just stick men . . . stick men . . . stick men . . . stick men . . . stick men . . . and even worse, a blind stick sorceress.

'Thank you for coming,' she said, sweetly, feeling Chico's face with her hands. 'It has been so long since I touched a real human face, you must forgive me.'

'I'm sorry I'm not a better drawer,' said Chico sadly. 'I did so want Fiddledy-dee to be perfect. I didn't mean to make you all so thin and rigid.'

'What's done is done,' she smiled.

'It was unforgivable of me to forget your eyes.'

'I probably would have done the same,' she said, softly. 'You had so much to draw in so little time.'

'Perhaps I should rub the picture out and do a better one,' he suggested.

'I'm afraid that won't work,' explained the sorceress. 'The enchanted forest can only be drawn once. The first time brings life, thereafter what you paint is only a picture.' The stick men courtiers turned their flat heads discreetly to one side as Chico's bottom lip wobbled. 'There is one way to change how we look,' murmured the sorceress quietly. Chico looked at her intently.

'How?' he said.

'It is written, that if a human being comes to live with the stick men, then the stick men shall become human beings.'

'Written where?' asked Chico. The sorceress chuckled.

'Well between you and me, I saw it scribbled on a

lavatory wall somewhere. But it's too much to ask of you, Chico.'

'Why?' he said, eagerly. 'It's not as if it would be for ever, is it?' The sorceress took her hands away from his face. 'Is it?'

'It's not a holiday job, I'm afraid.'

'Oh.' Chico's face fell. 'Then I can't do it,' he said. 'I can't leave my parents for ever. They'd never forgive me.'

'No,' agreed the sorceress. 'You're a good and dutiful son, Chico. They don't deserve you, but you're right to return.' But deep down inside, Chico knew that he didn't want to go.

Suddenly there was a huge commotion in the castle. A stick man messenger ran up to the sorceress and whispered in her ear. She nodded her head and turned to Chico.

'Your parents are home,' she said. 'They're looking for you. It's time you went back.' Peering out through one of the castle's windows, Chico could see his parents steaming in his bedroom.

'LOOK AT THIS!' screamed his mother, gawping at Stan's scribblings and the lop-sided picture of Fiddledy-dee. 'Look what the little rat has scrawled today!'

'I shall beat him when he gets home,' roared Chico's father.

'I've a better idea,' sneered his mother. 'Let's put him in a sack and drop him in the river.' Chico's father laughed.

'You are a brilliant woman,' he said. Then he left the

room for a moment and returned with a black bucket.

'You know, I wouldn't mind if he could draw,' said Chico's mother, peering in through the castle window, 'but have you seen these freakish stick men that he paints. Hideous creatures. Yeuch!'

'I agree,' said his father, throwing a steaming bucket of hot soapy water at the wall. The suds lifted the crayon off the paper and sluiced the picture down through the cracks in the floorboards. Chico and the stick men were washed away as the enchanted forest of Fiddledy-dee faded into obscurity.

But the story doesn't end there. The picture may have disappeared, but the magic continued. After all, Fiddledy-dee had been born of a sorcery far more powerful than a steaming bucket of hot, soapy water. Of course, it was now impossible for Chico to step out of a picture that didn't exist, but he was still able to live there; and because he was living there, the stick men turned into human beings, the sorceress regained her sight, the castle straightened up, the forest sprouted hundreds of new trees, the magic river flowed and the sun shone down on a land filled with laughter and birdsong.

But just as washing off the picture of Fiddledy-dee could not destroy the enchanted forest, so too, the rubbing out of Impey's helicopter sketch could not destroy the hobgoblin's black magic. Chico's parents were both killed in a bizarre flying crash three weeks later, in which their rotor blades clashed in mid-air. When their bodies were pulled from the sea, their heads had swollen to five times their normal size. They looked like stick men.

Chico still lives in Fiddledy-dee. Somewhere, in some town, in some street, in some house, there's a picture of a forest on a wall. It may have been covered up or painted over, but it will still be there. Put your ear to the wallpaper and listen for the tinkling of the magic river. If you hear it, try calling out Chico's name. In the dead of the night, when the owl swoops across the moon, he may come out with the stick men and pay you a visit.

Word of warning, though. Try not to wake the knobbly hobgoblins.

Little Fingers

There is only one thing a boy loves more than his mother and that is his thumb. Daffyd Thomas's thumb was a misshapen stump, sucked out of all recognition by his lick-lapping lips and powerful cheek muscles, puffy and white like a bloodless sausage, nailless and gnawed, with two raised welts on the knuckle where his front teeth pressed down on the bone.

Daffyd was never to be seen without his thumb in his mouth. He ate with his mouthful, he worked with his mouthful, he even spoke with his mouthful, which as you all know, is most impolite.

'I-uvt-tess-mmm-tum,' he mumbled through his bottle-stop digit, which roughly translated as, 'I love the taste of my thumb.' His mother couldn't understand a word he said. As far as she was concerned, the thumb had to go.

She painted the shrivelled nail with bitter aloes, and dunked the meaty bit in a concoction of her own brewing, made from sheep's bile, snail's ooze and crusty scrapings from a bluebottle's legs. It made Daffyd's thumb taste so disgusting that he couldn't bear to be in the same room as it, let alone suck it surreptitiously. Daffyd was cured.

However Mrs Thomas's suckless success brought with it a secondary problem. Deprived of its daily slurp, Daffyd's idle thumb soon became agitated and twitchy. It was bored stuck inside Daffyd's trouser pockets all day. It wanted to explore the world for itself. So Daffyd's thumb started fidgeting: playing with the buttons on the TV remote control while Daffyd's parents were trying to watch their favourite programme; picking Daffyd's nose and flicking it at the cat; ringing the neighbour's front door bell and then hiding behind Daffyd's back. Soon, however, Daffyd's fingers and non-sucking thumb became wildly jealous of the fun that the sucking thumb was having, and they joined in too, making Daffyd's hands the most probing, prodding, seeking, tweaking, twitching, scratching, poking, picking, pressing, messing, wiggling, twiddling, fiddling hands in the whole of Wales.

Daffyd's little fingers had the devil in them.

At breakfast, they drummed rhythms on the wooden

table, tapped out tunes with the cutlery on the milk bottle, and catapulted the teaspoon out of the sugar bowl.

'Daffyd!' scolded his mother. 'Look at the mess.'

'Sit on your hands, boy!' shouted his father, whose newly oiled hair was coated in a fine white cap of sugar granules.

'Sorry, Mam,' said Daffyd, but before the words had even passed his lips, his wandering fingers were off again. Boing-ing the butter knife underneath his thigh, crunching the cereal in its cellophane bag to locate the free plastic glow worm, shredding the paper napkin into a thousand tiny, flaky pieces. And after breakfast, while Daffyd stood by the front door waiting to go down the shops, his fingers snapped the letterbox flap up and down behind his back. Click, clack, click, clack, click, clack, click, clack, click, clack, click, clack, click . . .

'DAFFYD! FOR THE LOVE OF GOD, WILL YOU STOP THAT CLACKING NOW!' wailed his mother.

Fingers in the cake mix, fingers in the ink, fingers in the butter dish, fingers in the sink. Fingers in the video, frisbee-ing a hat, fingers in the hi-fi, fingers in the cat . . .

'That is dirty, Daffyd! How would you like that done to you?'

'Oh, sorry, Mam. I wasn't looking what I was doing! I thought it was a woolly glove.'

Fingers pulling loose threads out of jumpers, fingers knocking knick knacks off a ledge, fingers plucking stuffing out of car seats, fingers stripping leaves from dad's front hedge. Fingers leaving apples down the sofa, fingers peeling paper down the wall, fingers testing meat knives for a sharp edge, bloody fingers dripping through the hall.

'Daffyd! Please!' screeched his exhausted mother.

'But I'm dying, look you, Mam!' said her bleeding son.

'Well, it will serve you right for fiddling if you do!'

Daffyd's little fingers were a finger-clicking nuisance. Always on the sniff, always scratching, scribbling, scrunching and scraping, and always, ALWAYS irritating. His parents were persecuted by them day and night. And so it was, one day, that his mother announced to Daffyd, that she and his father were taking a holiday *on their own* to escape from the fiendish finger-fiddling.

'But who will feed me?' asked Daffyd, pathetically.

'Your Granny Gwyneth,' said his mother.

'But she's ninety-three,' exclaimed Daffyd. 'She set the kitchen on fire last time she boiled an egg.'

'She is also stone deaf, Daffyd, so she won't be bothered by your fidgeting,' said his mother, triumphantly. Then she went upstairs to pack her bags and order a cab for the airport.

Granny Gwyneth's idea of a busy day was to sit in front of the television and snooze. Daffyd couldn't leave the house in case she fell out of her chair or needed a digestive biscuit or her sixteenth cup of tea. He was trapped for two whole weeks, babysitting the babysitter. He couldn't even have a conversation with her, because she was as deaf as a post.

'Shall we go to the cinema today, Granny Gwyneth?' he asked, one morning.

'Oh I don't know, young Daffyd. I think Princess Di is lovely,' she replied, nodding her head slowly.

'No, the cinema. To see a film!' shouted Daffyd.

'Lovely,' croaked his aurally challenged nan. 'But I prefer cockles!' Daffyd twisted the curtain cord round his fingers and screamed a silent scream. There was a clatter from above as the curtain rail pinged out of the wall and descended on his head. 'Or jellied eels,' added Granny Gwyneth. 'I was always partial to a little snake in the basket!' For a boy with such active fingers, sitting on the sofa all day discussing woollen blankets and denture fixative was a living hell.

So great was Daffyd's boredom that he fidgeted with every object in the house fifteen times, and wore each of them out in turn. On the fourth day of his incarceration there was only one possession of his parents' left unbroken. The telephone. So he turned his hand to that. Lifting the receiver up and down like a tiny dumb-bell to set up a rhythmical clicking, tapping tunes on the tone buttons, and ringing up complete strangers with silly names.

'Hello, is that Mr Smellie?'

'Yes, who's this?'

'You're Smellie, are you?'

'I am.'

'Well I should do something about it then!'

And some days, while Granny Gwyneth gassed on about

pet food or foreign cheeses, Daffyd would just dial numbers at random to see who he got. He spoke to Buckingham Palace kitchens and ordered anchovy souffle with custard covered meatballs for the Queen's tea, he bought three jet fighters for the Saudi Arabian Air Force when he found himself connected to the Foreign Office, and he told a lady in Gwent that she'd just won half a ton of manure in a gardening competition and the lorry would be round in half an hour to dump it on her doorstep! He ran up a phone bill of two and a half thousand pounds, speaking to places as far away as Australia, America and the Balearics, but not once did his granny notice. The poor old duck never heard a thing.

'Now then, knitting!' she announced one day, leaving Daffyd groaning at the thought of it. 'There's a fine profession for a fit, young man, Daffyd. Knitting cardigans and bootees. Did I ever tell you that I once knitted a scarf for your father? A fine garment it was. Dirt brown as I recall. It shrank to the size of a sock when your mother washed it.' Daffyd picked up the telephone and punched in seven digits, in the hope that somebody interesting might answer. 'It was wrong of me I know, being a Christian lady, Daffyd, but I never forgave your mother for that!'

'Hello?' said a sing-song Italian voice at the other end of the line.

'Hello,' said Daffyd. 'Who's that?'

'It'sa Pizza Mafiosa, here. What you want?'

'A pizza,' said Daffyd, for want of anything better to say. Granny Gwyneth was nattering away happily to herself in the background about cross-stitching. 'What have you got?'

'We do all sorts at Pizza Mafiosa, my friend. There'sa the Meat Massacre, the Pepperoni Punch Up, the Shotgun Special, and thata comes with the extra knobbly kneecaps on the top if you like. We do a very nice Rabbit Punch, a Concrete Overcoat, thatsa quite heavy on the stomach that one, then there's a Kidnap Caper and a Chicken Execution, with a blindfold of course. They all come in a nice wooden box with a side order of horse's head in a garlic bed.'

'They all sound lovely,' slurped Daffyd. 'Would you recommend the Kidnap Caper?'

'Depends,' said the man. 'That's on our Children's Menu. Are you a child?'

'Yes, I am.'

'Good. You on your own?'

'Well apart from my granny.'

'Is she old?'

'Very,' said Daffyd.

'It'sa perfect. We can deal with her. And your parents, they rich?'

'I don't know,' said Daffyd. 'They've just gone on holiday, so I guess they must be.'

'OK. One Kidnap Caper on it'sa way,' said the voice. 'Don't move. Where is you?' Daffyd told the man from the pizza shop where he lived, put down the phone and licked his lips. He loved pizza. He could get his fingers nice and sticky.

When the doorbell rang, ten minutes later, Granny Gwyneth was reminiscing about the blitz in World War Two, one of her favourite topics of conversation.

'Those were the days, look you,' she smiled, dreamily. 'Singing songs in the shelters while the bombs burst overhead. Eating powdered eggs and bully beef sand-wiches. It was easier when there were rations. Had no choice, see.' Daffyd got up off the sofa, sneaked out of the sitting-room without his granny noticing and opened the front door.

'Buona sera, signore. Your pizza,' said the pizza delivery man, who was dressed in a smart, shiny suit and was wearing dark glasses.

'A Kidnap Caper,' salivated Daffyd. 'I can hardly wait, see! Where is it?'

The man had nothing in his hands.

'The van,' he grunted. 'Now!' And he produced a machine-gun from behind his back.

'Oh, the pizza's in the van, is it?' guessed Daffyd. 'Too big to carry on your own?'

'Shutta your mouth and come with me!' ordered the pizza delivery man, driving the muzzle of his gun into Daffyd's ribs.

'Whatever you say,' said Daffyd, setting off down the

front path towards a long, black limousine parked in the road. 'That's a very impressive vehicle,' said Daffyd. 'Most people round here deliver pizzas on clapped out motorbikes. Business good, is it?'

'Get in!' growled the man with the gun.

'But Granny Gwyneth, I've left her talking about the war—'

'In!' barked the Italian, ducking Daffyd's head through the open door and pushing him roughly across the back seat. 'One move and you're pizza topping!'

'So, how much is this pizza going to cost then?' asked Daffyd, as the limousine screeched away from the kerb.

'Everything your parents have got!' smiled the man from Pizza Mafiosa. 'Ciao for now, bambino!' Then he rifle-butted Daffyd across the side of his head and knocked the muddled Welsh whelp into the middle of next week.

Daffyd had been kidnapped.

The next day a ransom note plopped through the letterbox, but Granny Gwyneth didn't hear it. She was still sitting where Daffyd had left her when he went to the door to collect his pizza, still prattling on about the war to an empty sofa.

'Mind you, Daffyd, the nights were terrible cold and fuel was scarce. We used to burn rats to keep us warm, look you.' So the ransom note lay unopened, which was a shame, because it read:

* * *

*WE HAVE GOT YOUR SON. ENCLOSED IS
ONE FINGER TO PROVE IT. COME TO
PICADDILLY CIRCUS WITH £10,000 IN CASH
TONIGHT OR WE'LL CHOP OFF ANOTHER
ONE.*

   The Pizza Papa

In the envelope was Daffyd's little finger; stiff, cold and white.

The next day, another envelope dropped on to the doormat and was missed by Granny Gwyneth. She was still talking to herself. 'Did I ever tell you about the day Dai died? That was a sad, sad day, Daffyd.'

Another day, another finger. And so it continued for seven further days – Daffyd's fingers posted through the door at nine o'clock every morning and sniffed by the cat, while Granny Gwyneth wallowed in nostalgia in her comfortable old armchair, in the empty old lounge.

The deliveries would have carried on forever (until Daffyd had run out of fingers, of course) had not Mr and Mrs Thomas returned home from holiday. You can imagine how surprised they were to find their son's fingers on the doormat. You can imagine how surprised Granny Gwyneth was too.

'I thought he was in the room with me, so I did,' she cried. 'Sitting on the sofa!'

Mr Thomas paid the ransom immediately and Daffyd was returned the following morning.

'How are you feeling, Daffyd?' asked his father.

'Well not with my fingers,' said Daffyd, holding up his stumpy hands and wiggling his one remaining thumb.

'Still, look on the bright side,' said his mother. 'You won't be fiddling no more, will you, Daffyd?'

'Don't expect I will, Mam,' said Daffyd, slipping his lonely thumb into his mouth and comforting himself with a long, soothing suck.

'Oh Daffyd,' chided his mother, 'I'm very disappointed in you.' She slapped his wrist. 'I thought you'd grown out of that filthy habit, boy.'

'Get the bitter aloes, Mother,' said his da. And she went upstairs to the bathroom cabinet to do as she was bid.

Bessy O'Messy

Bessy O'Messy had a fine head of red, Irish hair that rippled down her back like peach melba, emerald green eyes that sparkled like a tumbling waterfall and a great big gap at the top of her neck where her brain should have been. She was the messiest girl it had ever been her mum's misfortune to meet. Her brain and her hands were completely unconnected. She'd put things down and immediately forget that she'd done it. Bowls of half-eaten cereal on the stairs, dribbling toothpaste tubes on the bookshelves in her dad's study and chocolatey Kit Kat wrappers stuck to the sofa like large red stamps. Her parents had learned that asking Bessy to help around the house was a dangerous thing to do. Like the time, for example, she was asked to empty the cat litter tray and left it on the welcome mat inside the front door (just perfect for treading in), or the time she abandoned the Hoover in the middle of the lawn (still sucking), or the time she forgot to post that really important letter (a Pools win no less) and left it chilling nicely at the back of the fridge.

But of all the rooms in the house, there was one which suffered Bessy's rampant untidiness more than any other. It was of course her bedroom. The bomb pit. A heaving mass of school books and empty ink cartridges, romance novels and comics, cans and crisp packets, posters and clothes, and more clothes, and more clothes and (yes, you've guessed it) even more clothes. When Bessy undressed at night she simply dropped her clothes behind her and forgot about them. Out of sight, out of mind. Off of body, on to floor. She shed her clothes like a snake sheds its skin, or a dog moults its fur, or a pig sprays its muck round its pen. As a result, her bedroom looked like a charity shop storeroom, piled high with soiled rags, a wall to wall clothing compost heap, full of niffy knickers, sweaty socks, scrumpled skirts, tangy trousers, mouldy mules, fetid frocks, crusty cardigans, barfing blouses, high jumpers and ponky plims. Bessy wasn't dirty, it's just that used clothes tend to get up and walk on their own when they're left unattended for too long, and Bessy's pile of abandoned laundry hadn't been touched for three years. It just grew and grew, like a polyester/cotton mix monster, until it was the size of a large, industrial septic tank.

Whenever Bessy's mother asked Bessy to clear it up, which she did at least fifteen times a day, Bessy would say, 'Of course I will, but I's just got to do this first!' Which meant no, she couldn't be bothered. Besides, if she tidied her clothes away into cupboards and drawers, how on earth would she ever find them again!

To make matters worse, Bessy's younger brother, Callum, was the model of tidiness. A neat little boy, who always wore a shirt and tie and would say things like, 'Can I help with the washing-up now, Mammy?' after meals, and 'Are you's sure I can't scrub the ring out the bath?' He was forever rinsing through the family's smalls and loved to do his own ironing. For Callum, there was no more pleasant way to spend his Sunday afternoon than to fold his clothes over tissue-paper to keep the creases nice and sharp. When their mum clapped her hands and announced that it was tidy-up time, Bessy would groan, but Callum would kiss his mother's cheek and thank her profusely, attacking the mess with a spirited song on his lips:

> Hooray, it's tidy-time again,
> It's time to tidy out my den.
> I shall scrub,
> Rub-a-dub,
> With a brush and a tub,
> 'Cause to scrub is pure Heaven!

* * *

Bessy loathed this song, just like she loathed her younger brother for being one of life's little helpers. Callum made her sick to her boots for being so perfect and making her look like a slovenly slob.

'I hates you, Callum, does you know tha'?'

'Aye. Is there a chance you might change your mind, there?'

'Never.' Bessy spread her toast with marmalade and put the knife back in the butter.

'Does you mind if I ask why?' asked her brother, wiping his lips with his napkin.

'Aye, I do.'

'Is it 'cause I's smaller than you?'

'I've got my reasons.'

'Is it 'cause I's Mammy's favourite?'

'Sure, you're not. You're just a goody-goody.' Bessy sprinkled crumbs on the floor as she crunched her toast.

'By the way,' he said, fetching the dustpan and brush and sweeping up his sister's mess. 'I'm hoping to do a bit of dusting after breakfast. Will you let me do your room, Bessy? I could tidy away all your clothes. There's an awful bad pong coming out of there.' Bessy glowered at him.

'That's why I hate you!' she said. 'There's never a moment goes by that you're not with a duster in your hand.'

'Tell me,' said Callum, picking a gob of marmalade off Bessy's sleeve, 'are all big sisters this much fun, or is it just you?'

One day, as you might expect, it happened. Bessy's mess mountain finally reached the bedroom ceiling. The walls bulged and the glass in the windows cracked as Bessy's clothes overfilled the room like a turtle in a snail's shell. The pile was so huge that a mountaineer would have found it tricky to climb. When Bessy's mum tried to wake Bessy for breakfast she needed all her strength to shove the door open half an inch.

'What's happened in here!' she screamed, squeezing her head and shoulders through the narrow gap.

'Bessy has,' said Callum smugly as he wriggled past his mum's legs into the pit. 'She's a pig, isn't she Mammy?'

'Yes she is,' she replied.

'Honk honk,' hooted Callum. 'But I's not, am I?'

'No, Callum you're not. Bessy, wake up!' There was a groan from the bed as Bessy opened her eyes.

'Who's there?' she yawned, unable to see a thing through the laundry wall.

'Mammy,' piped up Callum. 'Boy are you in trouble, you pig.'

'Watch who you're calling a pig, tidy-drawers,' warned Bessy, shoving her head over the top of the pile and grinning cheesily at her mum. 'Is there a problem?' she asked, innocently, knowing full well that there was.

'You'll clear this room up immediately!' seethed her mum.

'I was just going to,' lied Betty.

'Ooh, could I help?' drooled Callum, excitedly.

'No,' said his mum, tartly. 'It's Bessy's mess. Bessy will do it on her own.'

'Yes Mam,' sighed Bessy.

'And you's not to come downstairs till it's all done, mind.'

'Yes Mam.' Callum tugged at his mum's elbow.

'Are you's sure I can't help?' he pleaded.

'Be off with you!' shouted his mum. 'The pair of you's a flaming nuisance!' Then she slapped downstairs in her slip-on slippers, leaving Callum in tears and Bessy stuck on top of her pile of clothes with her head jammed against the ceiling.

'Will you give us a hand, here, Callum?' she cried. 'I can't get down.'

'No,' sniffed Callum. 'I's not allowed to help, remember?' Then he slammed the door and went to get his breakfast. Bessy was furious. Why couldn't she keep her room the way she liked it? She didn't mind the swarms of flies or families of moths that lived inside her clothes heap. It was good to have pets. No, she wouldn't do what her mum told her. It was *her* life. She could live like a pig if she wanted. She'd go back to bed, that would teach her mum a lesson. She tried to back up by wriggling her elbows, but the laundry pile held her fast like a giant patchwork straitjacket. She was well and truly wedged, like a fat cat in a mousehole. She'd have to go forward. She used her fingers to scrabble at the top layer of clothes and made a small hollow deep enough to free her arms, which were pinned by her sides. Then, like a large mole, she pushed the clothes in front of her to either side and edged forward towards the door. She'd got about halfway, when the pile of linen suddenly collapsed beneath her. She shot down through a hole the size of a dustbin lid, falling into a dark tunnel that seemed to have no bottom. She twisted and turned in the air, jumpers and skirts spinning around her head, as she plummeted downwards like a stone in a well. She landed with a bump on a soft bed of socks and brushed the hair out of her eyes.

'Agh!' she screamed. Then, 'Who's you?' Standing in front of her were six tiny men, no more than a foot high. They were dressed in green tweed suits and on their heads they wore conical caps, like acorns, with a feather poking out at the back. Their faces were wrinkled like old apples and the backs of their hands were as gnarled as twisted tree roots, but their fingers were long and smooth. Each was holding the reins of a miniature horse. Bessy stood up and towered over them like a skyscraper.

'Top o' the morning to you, missy,' said the one with the clay pipe sticking out of his mouth. 'And what would you be doing down here, might I ask?'

'I was going to ask you exactly the same question,' said Bessy. 'Where am I?'

'In the Land of Laundry,' said the one with egg dripping down his bristly chin. 'Allow me to introduce ourselves. O'Reilly, O'Reilly, O'Reilly, O'Reilly, O'Reilly and Rafferty, but we call him O'Reilly to avoid any confusion.'

'I'm Bessy,' said Bessy.

'And we's leprechauns,' said O'Reilly. 'The little people. Sure, you must have heard of us?'

'To be sure,' nodded Bessy, 'but what are you doing in me laundry?'

'Well, we'll let you in on a little secret,' said O'Reilly, 'so long as you promise not to tell a living soul.' Bessy promised.

'We likes a bit of a mess,' explained O'Reilly.

'In fact we likes a *lot* of a mess,' added O'Reilly. 'And when I saw your pile of dirty clothes, I said to O'Reilly here . . .'

'That's me,' said O'Reilly, bashfully.

'That's him, that's right, I said to O'Reilly, to be sure this is leprechaun heaven. We can live inside Bessy O'Messy's pile of linen, making as much mess as we like and nobody will ever notice.'

'And that's what we done!' said O'Reilly. 'Herbal tea bags!'

'I beg your pardon? said Bessy.

'Ah, don't mind him. He's a bit messed up in the head,

that's all,' winked O'Reilly, pointing his finger at his temple and giving it a twirl.

'We all are,' grinned O'Reilly. 'We's plagued by forgetting things, so we are. Top o' the morning to you, missy. I'm O'Reilly. And what might your name be then?'

'I'm Bessy,' said Bessy for the second time.

'Of course you are,' said all the O'Reilly's together. 'Top o' the morning to you, Bessy. We's leprechauns. The little people. Welcome to the Land of Laundry! Now what did you say your name was?' Bessy thought she was bad at remembering things, but the leprechauns appeared to have no memory at all.

'Shall we be going then?' asked O'Reilly.

'Where to?' said Bessy.

'I forget,' said O'Reilly, 'but I'm sure to remember when we get there.'

Then he disappeared through a small black hole underneath one of Bessy's jumpers, with all the other little O'Reilly's in tow. It was only then that Bessy noticed they'd forgotten to take their horses with them.

Bessy was amazed at what she found when she crawled underneath her jumper. The cramped laundry world opened up into a spectacular landscape – spectacular for its messiness. There was a crooked path in front of her that was littered with old wooden carts, rusty cookers, two jalopies, a table, three mattresses, a television (showing BBC1) and an assortment of bust-up bikes, some with wheels and some without. Two trees stood on either side of the path, their branches peppered with kites, bunting and twisted sheets that the leprechauns had once used for swinging on, but had long since forgotten about. A small pond to Bessy's right was clogged with prams and upturned boats. A picnic basket (still full of sandwiches and bottles of stout) floated lazily across its surface like a ghost ship. A barbed-wire fence enclosed what had once been a sheep pen, but was now used by the leprechauns as a weed garden. At least that's what Bessy thought it was, because it was packed to the wire with nettles and thistles and whiskery grass. At the end of the path stood the leprechauns' house, a ramshackle affair, with half a roof, no front door and, strung between the two top windows, a washing line laden with tea bags that O'Reilly had hung out to dry.

'There's no sense in wasting them,' O'Reilly chuckled in Bessy's ear.

'To be sure,' said Bessy. 'You've got yourself a beautiful home here, Mr O'Reilly. How long did it take you to decorate?'

'We sort of make it up as we go along,' said O'Reilly. 'There's no real plan, you understand.'

'If there was you wouldn't be able to find anything,' said Bessy.

'Precisely,' said Mr O'Reilly. 'You should see our beautiful kitchen.'

'In the house?'

'In the house, in the garden, there are bits and bobs in the bedrooms too, but we've lost the sink. I can't think where O'Reilly put it.'

'Well I think it's heaven,' gushed Bessy. 'There's nobody to tell you to clear it all up.'

'Shall we go inside?' asked O'Reilly, opening the white, wooden gate for Bessy to step through.

'Oh dear,' she said as the fence came away in his hand.

'Never liked it anyway,' chuckled O'Reilly and he threw it over his shoulder into the rose bush.

The inside of the leprechauns' house was Bessy bliss. Plates in the sink, food on the floor, the fridge door left open so the mice would have somewhere to sleep, pots and pans in the downstairs loo, comics strewn up the stairs, vests over the standard lamp, bits of old motorbike on the coffee-table and a family of chickens nesting in the sofa.

'Don't you just love fresh eggs in the morning,' said Bessy gleefully.

'Sure, you don't eat them?' said a shocked O'Reilly.

'Why? Don't you?'

'A terrible waste. We use them as bombs. They make a great splat on the forehead.' And with that, he slipped a freshly laid egg out from underneath the hen and threw it straight between O'Reilly's eyes. Bessy couldn't stop herself from giggling as the yellow yolk dripped down O'Reilly's nose and plopped on to the carpet.

The bedrooms were piled high with dirty linen (home

from home for Bessy), the beds were unmade, the curtains had been removed from their rails and used to wrap cheeses, the sink was saturated with soaking socks and the bath was full to the brim with Guinness.

'To be sure, us leprechauns get a terrible thirst, Miss Bessy,' explained O'Reilly.

'So where do you bath?' she enquired.

'What's a bath?' asked O'Reilly. Bessy pinched herself hard to check that she wasn't dreaming. The Land of Laundry was paradise. These leprechauns didn't care about anything, least of all being tidy. Bessy was as happy as a snuffling pig in truffles!

'So, will you be after staying a while?' said O'Reilly.

'Does you really mean that?' she gasped. The leprechauns nodded their heads. 'I could stay here for the rest of my life!'

'What about your family?' asked O'Reilly.

'Sure, they wouldn't miss me and I certainly wouldn't miss them!'

'Then it's all settled,' announced O'Reilly, wiping the drippy egg off his hand on to his trousers. 'You's one of us now!' And they shook on it.

Back in Bessy's bedroom, the door edged open and Callum crept into his sister's inner sanctum with a duster in one hand and a laundry basket in the other.

'Bessy!' he called, softly. 'Are you there?' There was no

reply. He shut the door behind him and rubbed his little hands with glee. 'Right,' he salivated. 'Now where shall I be starting?'

'I beg your pardon?' Bessy was dumbstruck. 'Could you say that again, please, Mr O'Reilly?'

'Did we not make it clear what we brought you here for?' asked the leprechaun.

'You did not,' protested Bessy.

'It's the memory, you see,' said O'Reilly. 'It's not what it was.'

'What's not what it was?' said O'Reilly.

'I forget,' O'Reilly replied.

'Your memory,' said Bessy, who had changed her opinion of the little people and was now finding them tiresome.

'That's it,' shouted O'Reilly. 'My memory. I've remembered. Did we not tell you we wanted a housekeeper?'

'If you's had, I'd never have come,' shouted Bessy.

'But we shook on it,' said O'Reilly. 'It's a deal.'

'I don't want to clean your house!' wailed the red-haired girl, with fire in her emerald green eyes.

'To be sure, but it needs looking after,' grinned O'Reilly. 'We're no good at doing it ourselves! You've seen the mess we make. We live like hogs, Bessy. We need someone to tidy us up!'

'But not me! I don't do cleaning.'

'Are you's saying you won't do it, then?' said O'Reilly, suddenly. His voice was blunt. His manner aggressive. 'Are you's breaking our agreement?' He spoke for all of the leprechauns. Gone was their jovial, devil-may-care bonhomie; they were angry. They closed ranks against Bessy and stared at her with cold, searching eyes. Bessy noticed that their fingers were twitching, like they were up to no good.

'I'm not saying anything,' she prevaricated, as she tried to decide what to do. The leprechauns took a step closer.

'Did we tell you we was meat eaters?' snarled O'Reilly. 'We likes to hold the meat in our hands and chew the flesh off the bone.' Bessy wasn't quite sure what he meant, but if he was trying to scare her, he had succeeded.

'We wants a housekeeper,' said O'Reilly. 'Is it going to be you, like we agreed, or not?' The leprechauns were peeling back the flesh on their long fingers revealing sharp stiletto blades underneath. 'Yes or no?' Bessy could feel the sweat running down her back. She had to make a choice.

'No!' she screamed and with one bound she pushed the little people aside, charged down the stairs and ran out of the house. She could hear the leprechauns shouting after her, the patter of their tiny feet as they clattered down the stairs and gave chase.

'Nobody crosses the O'Reilly's and lives to tell the tale!'

'You'll never make it back to your bedroom, missy!'

'We're gaining on you!' Bessy reached the end of the crooked path and came face to face with a solid wall of soiled linen. She couldn't remember which way to turn. 'Wait till we get our fingers on you!' came the cry from behind. She turned right. Up ahead she could see her jumper and underneath, the black hole which led back to the spot where she'd landed. She threw herself on to her tummy and wriggled across a tangled tank top to reach the opening, but the leprechauns were smaller than she was and could run faster through the overhanging laundry. They grabbed her ankles as she crawled through the hole, dug their needle fingers into her legs and dragged her back towards them, like a harpooned whale.

Suddenly the Land of Laundry shuddered, as if struck by a fierce earthquake. Clothes crashed around their ears like falling rocks and the leprechauns were hurled backwards, losing their grip on Bessy's legs. She struggled back towards the hole, but it had gone, covered up by a pair of coffee-coloured shorts. And the tremor had stopped. The leprechauns picked themselves up and walked slowly towards her as she lay helplessly on the ground. Their steel fingers glinted by their sides.

'All you's had to do was a little tidying up,' said O'Reilly. His wizened face broke into a smile. 'We can't let you go, Bessy. You knows that don't you?'

'The big people mustn't know we's here,' explained O'Reilly.

'But I won't tell them!' pleaded Bessy.

'We know you won't,' said O'Reilly, ''cause we's going to kill you!' And they would have done too, had not the Land of Laundry suddenly turned topsy-turvy and a huge jet of water crashed down on top of the leprechauns' heads, squashing them flatter than six soggy shamrocks.

Callum only discovered that he'd washed Bessy as well as all of her clothes after he'd done the ironing. He pulled her out of a white sock, which he'd just pressed. She was as flat as a piece of paper, only six inches tall (having shrunk in the wash) and her hair was bleached white.

'Look what you's done,' she complained. 'You washed me too hot. All me colours have run.' She flicked her albino eyes towards her younger brother. 'Still, at least, you saved my life,' she said, gratefully.

'And done your washing,' added Callum. 'It's taken me hours, so it has, and I haven't even started on the dusting yet!'

'I'll give you's a hand,' said Bessy. Callum's face lit up. 'Honest?' he said.

'No messing,' said Bessy. And she meant it as well.

Jack in a Box

There's a joke shop in Great Pessaries
Sells ventriloquists' accessories,
Like tongues and arms and eyeballs, if they've got 'em.
But they also sell a dummy
That's so lifelike, it's not funny,
'Cause it speaks without a hand stuck up its bottom.

The Honourable Jack Delaunay de Havilland De Trop
(called Jack by those who could get a word in edgeways)
was a privileged child with an undeserved title. He lived
in a huge mansion in the rarified rural air of Hampshire,
just outside Great Pessaries, a town of considerable beauty,

but for the influx of the newly wealthy with their mobile phones and disposable wives. Jack's parents were landed gentry, the Lord and Lady Delaunay de Havilland De Trop, whose lives were devoted to balls and banquets and charity functions. They hob-nobbed with the rich and famous, transforming their gardens into tented disco halls, or polo pitches or outdoor art galleries depending on which particular good cause they were supporting that week. They were social butterflies, passing their days in a never-ending twitter of small talk, laughing with royalty, consoling the poor, but never short of a word or a conversation for whomsoever should step through their front door. Living with his parents, Jack had picked up their habits. Talking incessantly about nothing of interest, chattering inanely to anyone who'd listen. In short, a boy who loved the sound of his own voice and thought that everyone was spellbound by what he had to say.

The family were at breakfast one day, discussing Jack's sister's birthday party.

'So I said to the vicar,' trilled Lady De Trop, sipping on her glass of champagne and stuffing her face with smoked salmon toast. 'I said to him, I said, the price—'

'You know Andrew?' interrupted Jack. 'The boy with the father with the wig and the mother with a false nose made of plastic?'

'I'm talking,' said Jack's mother.

'Andrew says that if you eat chicken in your hands it

tastes like chicken, but if you eat it off a plate it doesn't.'

'Your mother is talking,' boomed Lord De Trop from the far end of the table.

'I think I'd prefer it to taste like chicken, because I really really love chicken. Especially when it's cooked. I mean I couldn't eat it if its skin was still cold and full of feathers.'

'Jack! Be quiet!' roared his father. 'Speak when you're spoken to.'

'Did I tell you that I'm in the football team?'

'I said, speak when you're spoken to!'

'You are speaking to me,' explained Jack. 'They've put me in as striker.'

His mother howled. 'I'm trying to have a conversation!'

'I hope I score a hundred goals, because then I'll beat the school record.'

'Shut up!' roared his father.

'The record's ninety-nine. It would have been a hundred but the referee didn't give a penalty in the match against St Dunstans, apparently. I don't know. I wasn't there. It was in 1919. I've got a verruca, look!' And he took off his shoe and put his foot on the table. Lord De Trop brandished his rolled up newspaper like a club.

'Don't interrupt your mother when she's talking!' he growled. 'Right, my dear, please continue.' Jack sat in silence while his mother attempted to carry on.

'Well I can't remember what I was saying now,' she muttered.

'You were talking about Rosie's birthday party,' said Jack.

'Silence!' glowered his father.

'I was only trying to help,' sulked Jack. 'Can't anyone say anything around here without getting their head bitten off?'

'Oh yes,' restarted Lady De Trop, 'the vicar. I was telling him how expensive it is these days to—'

'It's really painful this verruca. Are you sure you won't look?' Jack's father exploded out of his chair and grabbed his son by the scruff of his neck.

'Out you go!' he ordered. 'You can come back in when you've learned not to interrupt grown-up conversations.' Jack was bundled out of the room into the hall where his sister, Rosie, was sitting at the foot of the stairs dressing her favourite doll.

'I'm so sorry,' apologised Lord De Trop to his wife, as he went back into the dining-room. 'That boy needs to learn some manners! You were saying?'

'They're talking about my birthday party,' said Rosie, as her father shut the door. 'I'm not allowed in.'

'I've got a verruca,' said Jack. 'Have a sniff.'

Jack never listened to a word anyone said. It didn't matter who was speaking, he'd butt across their conversation without turning a hair. Once he interrupted the Queen while she was in diplomatic conference with the Nigerian Ambassador. 'Basketball's brill! You'd love slam dunking,' he shouted at the top of his voice. 'You could sit on Prince Philip's shoulders! No actually, you wouldn't need to bother would you, because you're tall enough already, aren't you Your *High*ness!' The Queen was not amused and turned away only to find Jack's sockless foot plonked in her lap. 'Do you want to see my verruca?'

On another occasion, he'd asked the Prime Minister what he thought about slug farms while the PM was deep in conversation with the Chancellor of the Exchequer. 'Slugs make wonderful pets,' he said, producing three from his pocket and slapping them down with a gloop on the back of the PM's hand. 'Cuddly, aren't they? And not as slimy as you might imagine! Woops! One's just gone up your sleeve, sorry!'

And once, at a Highland Ball for Burns Night, he'd barged in on an intimate conversation between a fresh-faced debutante and her prattling beau, and had asked the young lady if she wanted to look up his kilt. 'Go on,' he grinned. 'I bet you're wondering what I've got up there!'

'Thank you so much,' she declined demurely, 'but we really must be going.'

'I've got a mouse,' Jack said. 'Mother and father wouldn't let him come to the party, so I've had to sneak him in.' Then he lifted up his kilt and produced his pet mouse from a pocket in his boxer shorts. At which the distraught debutante fled from the ballroom, followed by her fawning flame, and Jack moved along the line of guests to the next unlucky couple, like a mechanical arm on a factory floor.

'Do *you* like mice?' he said, interrupting a joke that the gentleman was telling. 'Mine can do somersaults if you give him a push. I don't think his back legs are strong enough to do it on his own. Did I tell you that I got eighty per cent in History?' The couple tried to shuffle away, but Jack pursued them across the dance floor, oblivious to their discomfort, and shouted aloud for the whole world to hear, 'So tell me, do you get verrucas?'

Something had to be done. His conversation was banal, his interruptions intolerable. He needed to be taught a very sharp lesson.

Lord De Trop decided that Rosie should have a children's entertainer for her birthday party, but Lady De Trop didn't know how to find one. So she rang up her close friend, the Contessa di Fuengerola and asked her advice.

'Darling,' purred the Contessa down the phone, 'there is only one children's entertainer, don't you know? His name is Mr Frankenstein.'

'He sounds horrible,' said Lady De Trop.

'The children love him. He is a very ventriloquist, yes!'

'A very *good* ventriloquist?'

'That's what I say, darling.'

'How do I get in touch with him, then?' asked Jack's mother.

'You don't,' replied the Contessa. 'He gets in touch with you.'

'That's a bit strange, isn't it?' questioned Lady De Trop. 'I mean, how can he possibly know when I need him?'

'He knows!' said the Contessa. The letterbox rattled in the hall.

'Hold on, one moment,' requested Lady De Trop, placing the receiver on the table and scurrying into the hall to retrieve the letter. Seconds later, the Contessa di Fuengerola heard Lady De Trop gasp and pick up the phone in a hurry. 'You'll never believe this,' said Lady De Trop, 'but a card has just come through my letterbox.'

'From Mr Frankenstein?' chuckled the Contessa.

'How did you know?'

'He doesn't miss a trick, darling. He wants the job.'

'Yes, but should I let him have it?'

'Can you stop him?' laughed the Contessa.

'What do you mean?' said Lady De Trop.

'Now that he's heard about Jack,' explained the Contessa, mysteriously.

'What?'

'Must go, darling,' chimed her friend. 'My jacuzzi is getting cold! Adios.'

Lady De Trop was left standing with the dead phone in one hand and Mr Frankenstein's business card in the other. It was printed in bold gold lettering.

* * *

MR FRANKENSTEIN –
CHILDREN'S ENTERTAINER
VENTRILOQUISM A SPECIALITY
MARVEL AT MY LIFELIKE DUMMIES.
YOU'LL BELIEVE THEY'RE REAL WHEN YOU SEE
THEM WALK AND TALK!
I also do CONJURING and BALLOON SHAPES,
(if you're sad enough to be impressed by that stuff)
REASONABLE RATES FOR BIG PARTIES OF
NOISY CHILDREN

At the bottom was a personal note to Lady De Trop:

*I am so looking forward to meeting Rosie and Jack. I've
heard so much about him. I shall be there on Saturday at
three o'clock.*
Yours
Mr Frankenstein.
*P.S. Please ensure that the lock on the sitting-room door is
in full working order, as I insist on complete privacy during
a performance.*

The party was in full swing when Mr Frankenstein arrived.
Hordes of five year old girls ran screaming through the
huge empty corridors of the house playing hide the thimble.
Jack was bored with Rosie's friends and was lurking on his

own in the sitting-room when the doorbell rang.

'You must be Jack,' said Mr Frankenstein, as the boy opened the door.

'And you must be Mr Frankenstein,' said Jack, taking a good look at the tall grey-haired man on the doorstep. He didn't look a bit like a children's entertainer, more like an undertaker in a Western. Trim, thin and hollow-cheeked, a hooked nose and little tufts of hair over his ears like rabbits' tails. 'What's that in your eye?' he asked, bluntly.

'A monocle,' said the entertainer. 'May I come in?' Jack opened the door wide to let Mr Frankenstein and his boxes of tricks through, just as Lady De Trop ran into the hall with her daughter's screeching party in tow.

'I'm so sorry I wasn't here to greet you!' she panted. 'We lost one of the girls in the attic. Is there anything—'

'What's in that box?' butted in Jack.

'Sssh!' snapped his mother. 'I'm talking, Jack. Don't be so ru—'

'It looks like a coffin.'

'Don't interrupt!'

'Do you use dead rabbits in your act?'

'Quiet!' hissed his mother, wringing her hands with embarrassment.

'That's my dummy,' explained Mr Frankenstein. 'Perhaps you'd like to help me set up, Jack?'

'Would you like to meet the birthday girl, first?' asked

Lady De Trop, forcing a smile. She pushed her daughter forward. 'Rosie, this is Mr—'

'Let's go,' shouted Jack, cutting his mother dead and setting off for the sitting-room. Mr Frankenstein apologised to Rosie for leaving so hastily and promised to see her later. He followed the rude boy through the crowd of leaping girls and stopped when he reached the doorway.

'Wait out here,' he said, 'and I'll call for you in a min—'

'Are you a good conjurer?' said Jack, slamming the sitting-room door on Rosie and her friends in the middle of Mr Frankenstein's sentence. 'Only I once saw a conjurer who was pathetic. You're not pathetic, are you? Am I going to guess how you do all of your tricks?'

'I'm a ven—'

'Ventriloquist, yes, I know, but you do tricks as well?'

'A few,' said Mr Frankenstein.

'Why are you bald?' asked Jack. 'You'd look much younger if you had hair. Why've you let it fall out? I've got a verucca. Bet you couldn't magic that away.' Mr Frankenstein laughed. 'What's so funny?' asked Jack. 'Have you just thought of a joke? I know a joke about a wide-mouthed frog, but it's not suitable for Rosie and her friends. I think they're boring!'

'Don't you ever stop—'

'Talking? No, why? Don't you like what I'm saying? Do you want me to talk about something else? Swifts can't stand up, you know. They fly all their lives. If they landed,

their legs would snap, because they're so weak and thin.'
Mr Frankenstein was waiting to speak.

'I meant, you're very bad at—'

'Interrupting? I thought I was rather good at it, actually.'

'I can see that,' said Mr Frankenstein, frankly. 'You
know, you'd make an excellent ventriloquist's dummy,
Jack. Never quiet, always shouting, never listening to a
thing that the ventriloquist says.'

'Sorry?' said Jack, distractedly. 'Were you talking to me?
I'm going to get a motorbike when I'm sixteen and start
driving lessons before I'm seventeen so I can take my test
on my birthday. Have you got a car? I bet it's a small one.
My father's got six.' Mr Frankenstein's ears burned from
Jack's tirade of senseless words, his cold eye twitched behind
his monocle and his right hand jerked towards the boy's
gabbling throat, but he caught himself just in time.

'Give me a hand with this box,' he said, as he placed the
oak coffin on the coffee-table and started to unscrew the
lid. As he did so, Jack heard a tiny, plaintive voice cry out,

'Help! Let me out! It's dark in here.'

'That's you, isn't it?' said Jack.

'I'm cold, so cold!' whimpered the voice.

'Is it?' replied Mr Frankenstein, sliding off the lid to
reveal a pint-sized wooden dummy with a leather face. At
least it looked like leather. Jack poked it on the cheek to
check that it wasn't skin.

'Ow!' squeaked the dummy, 'that hurt.' Jack was so

startled that he leapt backwards from the box and fell over
Mr Frankenstein's feet.

'Its lips moved,' he exclaimed, kneeling up and peering
into the box again. The dummy's eyes blinked back at
him. Its wrinkled face was alive.

'Pick me up!' it squeaked.

'How are you doing that?' gasped Jack, checking to
see if Mr Frankenstein's lips were moving, which they
weren't.

'Clever little devil, isn't he?' said Mr Frankenstein,
admiringly. 'And all my own work!' Suddenly, the dummy
sprang forward in its box and grabbed Jack's ears.

'Pick me up!' it screamed, wrenching a tuft of Jack's
hair clean out of his head. Up close, the dummy's teeth
looked like sharp sticks, its gums and lips were brown and
weathered, like an old shoe. Jack had seen something like
this before, in a book about a head shrinking tribe in New
Guinea.

'Get off me!' he screamed, but the dummy had crawled
out of its box and was sitting across Jack's chest with its
wooden legs around his neck and its clothes-peg fingers
holding on to the back of his head. Their faces were
touching.

'Run!' hissed the dummy.

'What?' said Jack.

'Get away before it's too late!'

'Why?' asked Jack, but the dummy never answered. Mr

Frankenstein had wrenched it away and stuffed it back into its coffin.

'Time for the birthday girl,' he declared. 'Open the door please, Jack.'

'But what did the dummy mean?' asked the small boy. 'Run from whom? Get away from what? There are one or two questions I'd like answered, Mr Frankenstein. Like, how could that dummy speak and move on its own?'

'That's a long story.'

'And why did it have a tear in its eye?'

'Well—'

'And why did it have stitches round the base of its neck?'

'If you'll . . .'

'Answers on a postcard, please.'

'. . . let me speak.'

'Not listening, Mr Frankenstein.'

'But—'

'La la-la la-la! Not listening, till I get some answers!'

'BE QUIET!' roared the entertainer. And Jack was quiet. There was a mad look in Mr Frankenstein's eye, a wild fury that was not to be messed with.

'For once in your life, listen! It's magic pure and simple,' he said. 'I came here today, because you, the Honourable Jack Delaunay de Havilland De Trop, have been chosen by the elders of the Black Circle to receive the knowledge.'

'To make dolls talk?' clarified Jack.

'In a manner of speaking, yes,' said the entertainer more calmly.

'Wow!' chuckled Jack. 'Magic powers!'

'Come secretly to this address tomorrow morning – come alone, mind – and I will pass on to you the ancient wisdom of speaking in other peoples' tongues.' Mr Frankenstein handed Jack a small white card.

'This isn't a joke, is it?' said Jack, reading the wording.

'No,' said the entertainer. 'It's a matter of life and death, Jack. Don't disappoint me.' Then he composed himself and went to the door. 'Come on in children,' he announced, cheerily. 'I'm ready for you now!' Rosie and her over-excited friends babbled into the room and sat down on the floor. While Mr Frankenstein locked the door to stop the dummy from escaping, Jack took one last look at the card and popped it into his top pocket.

'A joke shop in Great Pessaries,' he mumbled. 'I wonder what it means.'

The Joke Shop was in the old lane district of Great Pessaries – narrow medieval streets with overhanging roofs and crooked doors. Jack leant his bike against the grinning clown's face painted on the shop window and pushed open the door. A cackling witch doorbell announced his arrival in the empty shop.

'Hello?' he called out. 'Mr Frankenstein? It's me, Jack. I've come for my magic lesson.' But there was no reply. 'I'm not scared,' he said to himself, looking at the ghoulish masks and plastic severed limbs on the walls. Slowly, he edged through the cluttered emporium, past fingers with nails driven through them, past eyeballs dangling from rubber sockets, past rows of ventriloquist dummies, hanging lifelessly off meat hooks like a rack of dead boys in a butcher's shop. Their eyes seemed to follow him as he crept behind the dusty counter and headed for a small door that lead out the back. Something touched Jack on the neck. He swung round. 'Mr Frankenstein?' A spider on a piece of elastic bounded up and down on his shoulder. He puffed out his cheeks. 'You know, I once read a story about a joke shop owner who went mad living with stuff like this,' he said out loud. 'If he kept talking he was less afraid. The sound of his own voice was comforting.'

The back door creaked open as he nudged it with his elbow. 'Mr Frankenstein, I'm here for the magic! I expect you're in the cellar or something, preparing a potion for the ceremony, aren't you?' The back room was brightly lit by a single naked bulb that cast long shadows across the far wall. Jack laughed uneasily, as he glanced to his left and saw two cardboard boxes full of tiny wooden arms and legs. 'This must be where Pinocchio was made,' he joshed. 'I'd hate to have a wooden body. Think of all those worms living inside you, munching you hollow. Mr Frankenstein, where are you?'

Jack was starting to get scared. He was standing by a third box full of wooden bodies and he could hear a bubbling sound in the corner of the room, like a hundred goldfish tanks with oxygen pumps. 'I'll be off then,' he quaked, peering round the dusty shelves to see where the bubbling was coming from. His heart leapt into his mouth. Stacked against the wall were thirty or more glass tanks of formaldehyde and floating in each tank, suspended by a cat's cradle of wires, was a real boy's head, chopped off at the neck. Eyes and mouths closed, the leathery heads bobbed up and down in the mummifying liquid like apples in a barrel.

Suddenly, a light was switched on. A bright, fluorescent bulb lit up the tanks like a fairground stall and the heads came to life. Eyes blinking, mouths chattering, the room was filled with the underwater bubble-talk of thirty boys' voices urging Jack to escape, to run while he still had the legs for it!

Jack had seen and heard enough. 'I'm history!' he shouted. 'See you, Mr Frankenstein!'

'Looking for me?' said a voice from a room to the side of the tanks. Jack froze. Mr Frankenstein appeared in the cold, blue, neon light with a half-made ventriloquist's dummy in his hands. He was wearing a white apron and half-moon glasses and sewing a leather head on to the stiff, wooden body with a needle and thread. 'Well, chatterbox Jack,' he smiled, grimly. 'What do you think of my magic now?' Jack's terror set his tongue wagging.

'Lovely, very nice. Magic magic! I've got to get back or I'll miss my bus.'

'But you came on your bike,' leered Mr Frankenstein, laying down the dummy and taking two steps forward.

'Puncture,' stammered Jack, backing away. 'I got a puncture. I don't know, the state of the roads these days! Potholes everywhere. More holes than a golf course! Blimey, is that the time? This is a new watch, you know. My old one had a date, but I preferred the colour of this strap. What do you think? Do you like . . . *an axe*!!!' Mr Frankenstein had picked up an axe off the counter. 'I can stop talking if that's what you want!' begged Jack. 'I can sew up my lips. Go on give me the needle and thread. It won't hurt! Honest! Mr Frankenstein! NOOOOOOOOOOOOOOOOO!'

Rosie stood in the garden wearing her black dress. She was rocking backwards and forwards on a loose rock in the path and chanting softly, through barely moving lips.

'My brother, Jack,
Please come back!
My brother, Jack,
Please come back!
My brother, Jack,
Please come back!'

She had been there for weeks. Her parents stood at the

dining-room window watching her, sadly. Lord De Trop had his arm round his wife's shoulder.

'Poor Rosie,' murmured Lady De Trop. 'She just can't accept that he's gone.'

'I've bought her a present,' said Lord De Trop. 'A friend, if you like.' He broke away to his desk, while Lady De Trop shed a silent tear and Rosie's mournful lament drifted across the lawn like smoke from a smouldering bonfire.

> 'My brother, Jack,
> Please come back!'

'I was passing a joke shop in Great Pessaries and I remembered how much Rosie had enjoyed that ventriloquist at her party,' said Lord De Trop, returning to the window with an oak box, shaped like a coffin. 'Do you think she'll like it?'

'It's lovely,' smiled Lady De Trop, taking the ventriloquist's dummy out of its box. 'You know,' she said, quizzically. 'It's got something of Jack in its eyes, don't you think?' The dummy blinked. It would have said something too, if its lips hadn't been stitched up.